CHERRY BURIED CAKE

LYNDSEY COLE

CONNECT WITH ME:

LYNDSEY@LYNDSEYCOLEBOOKS.COM

www.facebook.com/LyndseyColeAuthor

BOOK DESCRIPTION

Stuck in a snowstorm is a nightmare . . . caught with a killer is deadly!

With the roads impassable and the power out, real trouble arrives at the Blackbird Bed and Breakfast. The shocking discovery of a body pits the stranded pastry workshop guests against each other as they eye one another with a hefty dose of suspicion and fear.

While whipping up delicious desserts with the guests, Annie examines every morsel of information that points toward a murderer. She follows the smallest drop of chocolate frosting, hoping it will lead to the killer.

But the killer is clever.

When Annie finds herself sandwiched between the murderer and no place to hide, there's a chance that she won't escape from this sticky mess alive.

1

Annie stared through the French doors of the Black Cat Café into a wall of whiteness. "You're right, Jason, closing early is the smart thing to do. No one will be coming in during this storm." She wrapped her arms around herself, chilled with the thought of what waited outside.

"If you procrastinate much longer, I'm afraid you won't make it home. This snow is piling up faster than Leona's pastries. I'll head home and get the fire going so it's toasty when you arrive." Jason gave Annie a hug, then stepped back and stared into her eyes. "Please don't wait too long. The weathermen are predicting a fast-moving storm but it's not supposed to wind down until this evening. If you don't leave soon, you might get stranded here."

"Getting stranded is *not* part of my plan. I sent Mom and Greta home a half hour ago. After I finish up here, I shouldn't be more than ten minutes behind you. Now, get going and get that fire started." Annie smiled at the man she'd said "I do" to and never once regretted her decision.

She began her last-minute chores—stacking dishes in the dishwasher and storing perishables in the refrigerator—before Jason was out the door. Relaxing by the fire with Jason, her faithful terrier Roxy, and their two cats was the best recipe for a snowy afternoon. The sooner she was done at the Black Cat Café, the sooner she could kick up her feet and snuggle with her husband.

The door closed behind Jason, leaving Annie alone in the café. She usually savored these alone moments but with the wind howling and the visibility nonexistent, she had a sense of urgency to be done and on her way. She rushed through the rest of her chores on auto-pilot. "There," she said as she surveyed the tidy café, her voice sounding tinny in her own ears, "at least everything is where it belongs."

Her phone rang and Annie grabbed it from the counter, glad that it had caught her attention and she wouldn't forget it here overnight. A quick glance at the caller ID made her hesitate for a moment before she answered her aunt's call. "Hello, Leona. I'm just about to close up here."

"Good. Danny just called and he's stuck at his latest remodeling job. He's not sure if he'll be able to make it home. I've got all these guests arriving for the pastry workshop with Chef Marcel LaPierre. Can you help me? Please? Please? Please?"

Annie paused. Her peaceful vision of watching the storm with Jason while it raged over Heron Lake was quickly disappearing.

"Please?" Leona said again with even more desperation in her voice. "It's the first workshop at our Blackbird Bed and Breakfast and it *can't* be a failure," Leona begged. "I can't do it on my own."

Annie sighed. "I'll come, but you have to call Jason and explain this change in my plans. He's expecting me home soon."

"Will do. He'll understand." Leona hung up.

She was probably right. Annie's husband had an understanding streak as wide as Heron Lake, but it didn't change the fact that Annie had just agreed to something she certainly didn't have her heart in. Not with a storm raging outside.

But, of course, she couldn't say no. Leona and Danny had only opened up the renovated Blackbird Bed and Breakfast on the first of the year and Leona had been stressing over this event for the last six weeks.

Annie hung up her apron, took one last look around the tidy café before she bundled up, and trudged toward her car. She bent her head into the wind and clutched the top of her jacket closed so the snow couldn't blow down her neck. It was worse out than she'd expected with the snow reaching three quarters of the way up to her knees already. With bare hands, she wiped the snow off her windshield and climbed inside, blowing on her frozen fingers.

With the heat blasting, Annie warmed up her hands before she headed to the road. Her hands gripped the steering wheel with knuckles as white as the snow outside as she slowly followed the single plowed lane out of Catfish Cove.

She passed cars stuck in snowbanks on the side of the road but didn't dare stop to offer assistance for fear of getting stuck herself.

After what felt like an eternity, the lights for the Blackbird Bed and Breakfast glowed through the falling snow. Leona's neighbor, Randy Berry, tooted his horn as he pulled out of Leona's driveway and turned his plow truck toward his farm up the road.

Annie took a deep breath and forced her muscles to relax. At least she'd made it in one piece. Unfortunately, as she watched the snow pile up outside her car, she had the sinking feeling that she might be stranded here for at least this Friday night. She texted Jason to let him know she had arrived safely.

Through the blowing snowflakes, Annie saw the front door open and Leona wave to her. She grabbed her shoulder bag and made a mad dash into the warm bed and breakfast.

Leona wrapped her in her arms. "Were the roads terrible?"

"Horrible," Annie replied. "There's not much chance I'll be leaving tonight." She raised her head and sniffed the air. "What do I smell?" Leona's food provided the only bright spot in Annie's immediate future. She was starving.

Leona grinned. "I've been cooking up a storm for these guests. I hope they appreciate all the work."

"I thought this was a pastry workshop for the attendees to do the baking with Chef Marcel."

"Well, yes, sort of." Leona pulled Annie into the kitchen. "Chef Marcel will be teaching the basics for some French pastries but I'm providing the meals." Annie looked at Leona. "It's very intimidating having him here. What if he criticizes my cooking?"

Annie rolled her eyes. "Don't worry, Leona. You have your following in town. You're an awesome cook. Look at it this way— what if you don't like *his* cooking?"

Leona laughed. "I never thought of that. Here, you can take the drinks out and I'll introduce you to the guests. Everyone, well, except one person who I haven't heard from yet, is in the living room enjoying the fire. I need to keep them distracted from the weather."

"Oh?" Annie picked up the tray with coffee, tea, cream, sugar, and cups.

"There's been some anxiety about the storm. Some of them want to leave."

Annie raised her eyebrows. "That's not going to happen unless they want to spend the night stuck in a snowbank."

"That's what *I* told them, but at least some of them have no idea how bad it is out there." Leona leaned closer to Annie's ear. "Let's hope the power doesn't go out or I'll have a terrible panic going on here." She gave a little shove to get Annie moving through the kitchen door.

Before Annie pushed through the swinging kitchen door that led into the dining then to the living room beyond, she said, "You might have to offer alcohol instead of coffee and tea if you want them to relax."

"We'll see." Leona reached around Annie and opened the

door. She led the way to her guests. "Here come some refreshments everyone."

"Finally," the oldest man in the room grumbled. He eyed what Annie had on the tray as he twisted the end of his mustache. "Is *that* all you have? I thought that when I booked this place you would at least provide us with something decent."

"Chef Marcel, this is Annie Hunter," Leona said, ignoring his rude comment. "I'll be right back with some finger food."

"Finger food? What are you serving—chicken wings and potato chips?" He wrinkled his nose, suggesting there wasn't much worse than eating Leona's offerings even before he knew what they were.

A gray-haired woman stood and walked to the side table where Annie set down the tray. She was a few inches shorter than Annie and about thirty pounds heavier. "Don't mind him," she whispered. "I think he's a little rattled because of the storm. Plus, he admitted to all of us that his new cookbook is delayed. You know how these creative types can be—very dramatic and emotional." She held her hand out and smiled. "Connie Cook. Glad to be here."

Annie shook Connie's hand, a strong grip. At least one pleasant guest, Annie thought, which was better than nothing.

"I can't wait for the lesson on making éclairs." She handed Annie a brochure for the weekend workshop with glossy photos and a signed message to Connie from Chef Marcel. "That's one of my favorite desserts and Chef Marcel said he has a secret method to show us." Connie rubbed her hands together before she helped herself to a cup of coffee. Black. "Come on over and I'll introduce you to everyone else."

As Annie walked by a chair, Trouble, Leona's slate gray kitty, dashed out and attacked her feet. "Hey there, Mr. Troublemaker." Annie picked up the squirming ball of fur. "You need to behave yourself."

Connie laughed. "He has terrorized my poor Buddy." She

pointed to a brown dachshund sitting on the end of the couch next to a woman about ten years younger than Connie. "He won't even look at Trouble. Buddy has attached himself to Sarah here."

"Hi. Sarah Walter, and that's my husband," she pointed to a man sitting near the fireplace, "George."

Annie said hello.

"And over here," Connie pulled her to the edge of the room, "is Robin. Her mother gave her this workshop as a gift. Wasn't that such a great idea?"

Annie looked at Robin whose attention was on her phone and couldn't be bothered to look up. Annie wasn't sure it was a great idea or not. Time would tell with that.

"And there's one more person who hasn't arrived yet," Connie said. "Phil something or other. I hope he hasn't had a problem with the roads."

Annie thought of all the stranded cars she had passed on her way to the Blackbird. She had all-wheel-drive, but for people not used to how treacherous the winter roads in Catfish Cove could be, it might be a different outcome.

Leona returned with a tray artfully arranged with crackers, cheese, dips, and veggies, plus steamed asparagus wrapped in ham. "Here we go with something to tide you over until dinner is ready."

"I need a drink," Chef Marcel mumbled, "not a few crackers with cheese."

Annie saw Leona's jaw clench. She didn't know how long before Leona lost her control and lashed out at Chef Marcel's rudeness.

"If *that's* the best you can do, I'm demanding a refund." He leaned against the wall next to the fire with his arms crossed and a scowl on his face. Even his mustache drooped toward his chin.

Leona set her tray next to the coffee and slowly turned toward Chef Marcel. "Let me remind you that you signed a contract, Mr.

LaPierre, and there are *no* refunds." She stared at the chef with daggers shooting from her eyes straight to his chest.

"It's *Chef* Marcel, and if you don't provide what you promised, the contract is null and void. Read the fine print."

Leona's nostrils flared, but before she could respond or Annie could intervene, Leona's phone rang.

She answered. "Yes, Detective Crank?"

That got Annie's attention *and* curiosity.

"I see," Leona said. "Thanks for your call."

Leona, wide-eyed and pale, looked at the others who were all staring at her. "That was Detective Christy Crank from the Catfish Cove Police Department." She cleared her throat. "She was confirming that I had a reservation for Mr. Phil Hanks based on the brochure found in his car. Apparently, Mr. Phil Hanks will not be making it to the workshop tonight."

Chef Marcel threw his arms in the air. "What else could go wrong? A blizzard, terrible food, and now this? My whole agenda has been thrown out of whack."

"There's more, I'm afraid," Leona continued, her face a shade closer to the snow outside than to her normal healthy complexion. "Mr. Hanks won't be making it at all . . . he was found dead in his car."

2

Robin looked up from her phone. Her mouth hung open. Apparently, her ears *did* work.

Sarah looked at her husband. Fear replaced her bored expression. George remained stone-faced.

Connie swooned and managed to land on the couch instead of the floor.

Buddy woofed and jumped into Connie's lap.

Trouble hissed and darted under the couch at the dog's sudden movement.

Annie came to the rescue with the first distraction she could think of. She popped the cork on a bottle of wine. "I think we all could use something a bit stronger than coffee at a time like this." She filled glasses and served them to the guests.

"Finally, someone with some sense," Chef Marcel said. He threw his head back and drained his glass. "Refill." Without moving from his spot next to the fireplace, he held his glass out toward Annie like she was his personal servant and should be thankful for his presence.

Annie ignored Chef Marcel for the moment. She opened another bottle and poured two more glasses, one for Leona and one for herself. As she handed a glass to Leona, she whispered, "What do we do next? These people are about to revolt."

Leona set her glass on a small table. "Chef Marcel? Didn't you have your introductory session scheduled for tonight? I don't see why we can't keep on schedule. Once we've had dinner, you can take over my kitchen and present your first pastry lesson."

At the mention of food, color returned to Connie's cheeks. "Éclairs?"

"Well, since we're *stuck* in this place, I guess that's all we can do. Let's hope nothing *else* goes wrong."

"Great." Leona pasted on a smile. "Until dinner is ready, help yourselves to the appetizers and wine." Leona got Annie's attention and nodded toward the kitchen. They left the living room together.

Leona slouched against her work island. "This is a disaster. That man insults me with every word he utters. I don't know if I can keep myself from strangling him."

"Poison would be more appropriate for a chef than strangulation, don't you think?" Annie snickered and was rewarded with a snort from Leona. She opened a third bottle of wine and filled a new glass for Leona. "Here. We have to get through this night somehow so let's try to relax and focus on getting your dinner on the table."

"This night? He's here until Monday morning which means two full days of his wretched attitude." Leona sipped her wine.

"Maybe once he gets going with his teaching he'll lay off the insults. I think everyone is just a tad stressed because of the storm. After your delicious dinner and more wine, emphasis on the wine, we can turn the rest of the night over to the chef."

Leona took another sip. This one was bigger than the first. "I'd better not chug this down or I'll burn my chicken cordon bleu and forget to make my salad." She giggled. "At least then Mr. La-di-da Chef Marcel will have a legitimate complaint."

"We could put hot pepper flakes on his meal," Annie suggested.

"Or douse it with salt."

"Maybe burn his piece of chicken but cook everyone else's to perfection."

"I've got it," Leona grabbed onto Annie's arm, "I'll smear some of Trouble's chicken pate on the chef's portion."

"Or none of the above," Annie said. "It's fun to speculate, but you *do* want good reviews and repeat customers, don't you?"

Leona pulled her glass dish with the prepared chicken cordon bleu from the fridge and added the rest of her dinner ingredients to her work island. "You're right, Annie. I can't think about revenge when the customer is always right." She sighed. "Can you set the table while I get all this going?"

"No problem." Annie left Leona to what she did best and headed into the dining room. Soft music played in the background along with the muted tones of conversation coming from the living room. She opened Leona's hutch for the winter snowflake china which paired well with the woven red placemats. She set five places for the guests. She and Leona would serve, then eat later.

She opened the drawer for the silver and heard footsteps behind her.

"Annie?"

Annie turned around. "Robin. How can I help you?"

"I'm not feeling great. Do you think I could get a tray of food to take to my room instead of eating down here?"

"I suppose so, but don't you want to be part of the conversation? That's an important part of a workshop like this, to hear what everyone's specialties are, secret ingredients, and stuff like that?"

"Not really. My mom," Robin rolled her eyes, "gave me this workshop as a gift. I guess she's hoping I'll figure out what I want to do with the rest of my life or something like that. But I know cooking is not my future."

"So you don't even want to be here?"

"The bed and breakfast is awesome but as far as Chef Marcel," she rolled her eyes again, "is concerned, I'd rather stick pins in my eyes than spend another minute with that old creep. Have you noticed how he either ogles all the women or insults them? He's a narcissistic pig."

Everything Robin said was true, more or less, but Annie wasn't sure she'd be quite as harsh with her description of the chef as Robin was. It was going to be a long weekend and the more people engaged, the better to dilute the chef. "You should give it a chance at least. You never know what might inspire you this weekend."

"You sound like my mom. I know she worries about me but she shouldn't. I've got a plan, it's just that she doesn't like it." Robin placed her hands on her hips. "The food? I'm entitled to eat, aren't I?"

Annie sighed. "Of course you are. Come on into the kitchen and I'll round up something for you since diner isn't ready you. You'll have to come back down for dessert though."

Robin shrugged. "That's okay."

Annie scratched her head. "I'm starting to think your mother made a huge miscalculation by sending you here to a pastry workshop."

"Right? But I plan to enjoy the weekend anyway. Snowed in. Away from home. What more could I ask for?"

Annie led the way into the kitchen. Why did Robin even agree to come to this workshop if she wasn't interested? She pushed the door open and let Robin enter first. "We've got a hungry girl here, Leona."

Leona, with a white apron covered with blackbirds, straightened with a casserole hot from the oven. "Robin. How's it going?"

Robin scrunched her pierced lip to one side. "You're friends with my mom. What did *she* tell you?"

Leona set the casserole on the counter and shook the oven mitt off her hand. "She told me to keep an eye on you and make sure you enjoy the weekend."

"And?" Robin's eyebrows ticked up.

"And to make sure you learn how to bake at least one thing without setting the smoke alarm off." Leona grinned.

Robin picked up a buttery roll from a wicker basket, pulled off a chunk, and stuck it in her mouth. "Oh, I plan to learn something, all right. But I'm not sure it's what my mother is hoping for."

"Oh?" Annie leaned on the counter with her arms folded over her chest. "It's a pastry workshop. If you aren't planning to make éclairs and croissants, what's on *your* agenda?"

Robin popped the rest of the roll into her mouth and chewed slowly while a grin spread across her face. "I like that you ask, Annie. That's not something my mother has learned how to do. What do I want to learn?" She looked from Annie to Leona. "You see, what my mother can't seem to get through her head is that I don't want to learn to bake, I want to be a writer."

Annie felt her forehead wrinkle and noticed Leona nodding. "Interesting. So, this weekend is going to be a study in characters?"

Robin smiled broadly. "Exactly. I watch and listen and learn. What better location than a beautiful bed and breakfast to be stranded at? I think there's so much potential here for my first novel."

"Thanks for the beautiful compliment but . . . you'll change the name, won't you?" Leona asked.

Annie saw Leona's mouth turn down. With all the problems on the first day of her first big exclusive event, ending up in a novel might not be her idea of a positive endorsement.

Robin flicked her wrist dismissively. "Of course. I'm talking fiction so this just provides the inspiration for my ideas." She tapped her head. "I've got so much already, I can't wait to find out how the rest of the weekend goes."

"And all the guests? They'll be in your novel, too?"

Robin laughed. "Bits and pieces will be. For instance, Chef Marcel is such a blow-hard, full-of-himself fake and Connie is the stereotypical grandmother taking care of everyone. Although, it could be just an act. Sarah and George have some issues in their relationship that I haven't completely figured out yet, but if George pushes her enough I think she'll snap and let him know exactly what she thinks about him forcing her to come this weekend."

Annie's jaw dropped. "You certainly have learned a lot in a short amount of time."

"Yeah," she said proudly. "I'm young, and while I'm quietly sitting in the corner everyone assumes I'm not paying attention . . . but I don't miss much." Robin smirked.

"You left out your observations about two other people here." Annie raised one eyebrow as she appraised Robin.

"Yes. I did." She nodded her head back and forth as if she was trying to come to a decision as her eyes scanned the kitchen. "It's always harder to tell people to their faces what I've observed."

Annie forced a smile on her face. "Go right ahead. I'm sure your observations will be enlightening."

Robin's eyes darted to Leona who stood staring at her. "Okay. Well, you know my mom, Leona. She told me you can be blunt and outspoken."

Leona's mouth opened but she shut it as Robin put her finger up.

"Let me finish. It's true, but I don't say that in a bad way. You speak your mind with an honesty that I, at least, find refreshing."

Leona nodded. "Thank you . . . I guess."

Both Robin and Leona now turned their attention to Annie.

"Annie?" Robin said. "You're more complicated. You tend to

find yourself the mediator, jumping in to smooth over potential problems. Am I right?"

Annie nodded. "I guess you are." Was that a bad trait?

"So, you keep your true feelings masked. To a degree, anyways." Robin shrugged. "At least that's my observation based on a limited amount of time here. How about that food? I need to get up to my computer and work on my characters."

Annie searched in the refrigerator and found leftover beef stew with plenty of carrots and potatoes. She scooped some into a bowl and heated it in the microwave. "This ought to hold you over for now. And help yourself to some salad over there." She handed the bowl of stew to Robin and pointed to a stack of wooden salad bowls next to Leona's spinach salad.

As she scrounged up the food, Annie thought about Robin's ability to zero in on someone's character quirks so quickly. It was a bit unnerving, to say the least. "What do you want to drink?"

"Water's fine." Robin added a couple more rolls to her tray and a pat of butter. "This looks good. I'll probably be down when I get my writing done. Can I take these stairs?" She pointed to the back stairway that led from the kitchen to the upstairs.

"Sure. Are you trying to avoid bumping into anyone?"

Robin chuckled. "Exactly." And she was gone.

"I didn't see *that* coming," Leona said. "When her mother signed her up for the workshop she told me that Robin is a quiet, introverted girl. She's worried about her ever figuring out a path forward. She had such high hopes that Robin would be inspired by this French chef and begged me to nurture her along."

"She couldn't have been more wrong about her daughter," Annie added.

"Robin's mother told me that something like this workshop was what *she* had always wished she had done when she was younger. Too bad she didn't do it herself so she didn't feel compelled to force her lost dreams on her daughter."

"I'm sure her mother won't look at it this way, but Robin has already gotten quite a bit out of her first day here. I find her observations of the attendees, and the two of us, thought-provoking," Annie said. "I'll be doing my own observations from a new perspective tonight." She turned her head. "Do you hear something?"

Leona cocked her head. "It sounds like pounding on the front door."

Annie gave Leona a puzzled look. "Who could be here in this storm?"

3

Leaving Leona to tend to her cooking, Annie hustled to the front door. The pounding grew louder as she got closer. Anxiety flooded her brain.

She cupped her hands around her face and peered through the small window on the side of the front door. Even with the outside light on, all she could see was white. She cracked the door and peered out, then pulled it open the rest of the way.

Cold air and snow blew in behind a tall walking snowman who stepped inside. "Thank you. I thought I was destined to freeze to death tonight."

Annie blinked, trying to clear the mirage from her eyes. "How did you even get here?"

"Do you mind if I hang up my coat and warm up before I get into the details?"

Annie nodded and watched the man's mouth move as bits of snow fell from his face. He dropped a small backpack on the floor before he slowly unwound a navy-blue scarf from around his head. He pulled his arms out of the sleeves of his parka and stuffed the scarf, along with a matching hat and gloves, into the sleeve before he hooked it on the coat tree. When he pulled his feet out of his boots, a small snowdrift landed on the floor.

"You walked here?" Annie asked.

"Not exactly." He rubbed his hands together. "Do I hear a fire crackling?"

This wasn't part of the plan for the weekend, but what was Annie supposed to do? Send this poor guy back out into the blizzard? "Yes. Come on in." Annie held her hand out. "I'm Annie."

"Alex Harmon." He took Annie's hand in both of his. "I owe you my life, Annie."

They walked into the living room and four pairs of eyes turned as one to see the newcomer. Buddy barked.

Chef Marcel threw up his arms. "Who is this intruder? What is going on here? I thought I had the whole bed and breakfast for only *my* group. It's one of the reasons I chose this place—small and intimate. No distractions or nosey people butting into my workshop."

Annie clenched her jaw and ignored the chef's remark. "Everyone? This is Alex Harmon."

The chef frowned, making his displeasure obvious.

Annie ignored the chef and continued, "Apparently, somehow Alex stumbled to the Blackbird's front door in this storm." She quickly told Alex everyone else's names.

"You'll give him a room, won't you?" Connie asked. "After all, there is one room available now, after . . ." Connie didn't finish her thought about poor Phil Hanks who died before arriving.

"Yes, well, um," Annie stumbled for the best words to explain the free room to Alex. "Connie is right. There is a room available."

"Thank goodness," Alex said. "But I'd be willing to sleep on the couch if necessary. I don't want to put anyone out."

"Too late for *that*," Chef Marcel mumbled loud enough for everyone to hear. He refilled his wine glass. "I hope there's no shortage of wine to get me through this disastrous weekend.

"Wine. Perfect," Connie gushed. She filled a glass for Alex, took his arm, and moved him closer to the fire. "You look like you almost froze to death."

"Well, I thought that would be my fate until I saw the light shining through the snow. This storm caught me by surprise as I was heading north through town."

Connie patted his arm. "No need to worry about that. This Blackbird Bed and Breakfast is lovely. I think dinner is almost ready. Is that right, Annie?"

"Leona is working on the finishing touches. I'll go and help. Just keep feeding the fire to keep it toasty warm in here and I'll call when the food is on the table."

"I hate to be a bother," Alex said.

"Too late for that," the chef mumbled again before he drained his wine.

Annie stopped and faced Alex.

"If you were serious about finding a room for me on such short notice, could I bother you to show me the way?"

"Oh, of course." She didn't have anything more important to do, she thought sarcastically.

"I'll just get my backpack first so I can change into some dry clothes."

Annie led Alex upstairs to the room that had been reserved for Phil. Should she tell him what happened?

"From Mr. Marcel's comments, I'm surprised you have an empty room," Alex said, forcing Annie to make a quick decision.

"This room was reserved but . . . there was an accident . . . which led to a cancellation." She opened the door and gestured for Alex to go in.

"This is charming."

Annie had to agree that Leona performed some decorating magic making each room unique and comfortable. "You have a private bathroom through that door," Annie pointed to a pocket door next to the bed. "Dinner is just about ready if you would like to join us."

"Thank you for the invite, but I got the distinct impression that the chef doesn't want anyone crashing his party." Alex grinned. "Maybe I could trouble you for something later?"

"Don't let Chef Marcel keep you away from the dining room. I think the more the merrier." And the more to dilute that annoying man, she added to herself.

Alex nodded. "All right, then. Thank you."

Annie started to pull the door closed until Alex's question stopped her.

"What happened to your guest that was supposed to stay in this room? You said there was an accident?"

Annie hesitated but decided on the truth. "All I know at this point is that he was found dead in his car which was stuck in a snowbank. The detective from the Catfish Cove Police Department called us after she found the brochure for this workshop in his car."

Alex's eyebrows disappeared under his shaggy dark hair and his hand covered his mouth. "Oh dear. That could have been my fate."

"How did you find us?"

"Once the storm had me boxed in, I looked for accommodations on my phone. Fortunately, I wasn't too far from here so when my car got stuck in a snowdrift, I decided to walk the rest of the way. In hind sight, it almost became a deadly decision."

"But you made it."

"I did, but honestly, I had almost given up when I saw your lights."

Annie nodded. "Come down when you're ready." She closed the door and rushed to the kitchen.

"Where have you been?" Leona asked with panic in her voice. "Was someone actually at the door?"

"You won't believe it. This guy, Alex Harmon, got stuck in a snowbank and walked here. He's upstairs in the room reserved for Phil. Chef Marcel had another meltdown when I brought Alex in by the fire." Annie peeked under the foil covering Leona's chicken cordon bleu. "Your dinner is making my salivary glands work overtime and my stomach is begging for a taste. Is it about ready?"

Before Leona could respond, the door into the kitchen swooshed open. "There is a problem," Chef Marcel announced.

With dinner forgotten for the moment, Leona and Annie followed the chef into the living room.

Connie was slumped on the Queen Anne chair in the corner, closest to the fireplace.

The living room, overheated from the roaring fire, forced Annie to unzip her own fleece vest and fan her face. One look at Connie's red face let Annie know that at least the older woman was alive.

Sarah crouched in front of Connie, fanning her with a folded paper. "Connie, honey, can you hear me?"

Connie moaned and her eyelids fluttered.

Annie poured a glass of water. "Here," she handed it to Sarah, "try to get her to sip this. She looks overheated with all those layers on. It must be close to ninety degrees in this corner near the fireplace."

Leona propped open the door between the living room and the dining room and the door leading into the kitchen to let the heat circulate better.

"Oh my goodness," Connie moaned. "I think the wine got to me. It was a bad idea to drink that second glass on an empty stomach." She unbuttoned her wool sweater and flapped the two sides. "I'm starting to feel a bit better."

Buddy scratched her leg and whined.

Sarah picked up the dachshund and placed him on Connie's lap where he immediately licked her face.

"Disgusting. You cannot come near my food with those dog

germs slathered on your face," Chef Marcel said with a grimace. "I'll never be able to find my focus to teach *anything* to this group. That is, if there's even anyone left at the rate people are either dying, fainting, or just plain disappearing to their room."

George, who had been sitting quietly on the couch, snarled at Chef Marcel, "You'll owe us a hefty refund if you don't get your act together and deliver your course as promised. I paid for two for this event and you'd better come through." He read from the French Pastry Event brochure, "*Master Chef Marcel will share his secrets of the world of sweets which returns you to your carefree childhood.*" George looked up. "That's a pretty hefty promotion along with your promise that attendees will master the intricacies of making a perfect éclair, sweet petit fours, and much, much more."

The color in Chef Marcel's face drained away to the likeness of an éclair filling—pale yellow. "Of course, I am under unexpected duress with this," he waved his arm through the air, "this less than perfect environment."

George huffed and glared. "I don't like excuses." He looked at Leona. "I guess dinner will be delayed? I'm going to my room to clean up. Come on Sarah." George walked to the doorway without looking to see if his wife was following. She was.

"Oh dear," Connie sucked in a deep lungful of air. "I'm so sorry. I guess that wine went right to my head. Could you help me to my room? I think I want to rest for a bit before we eat."

Leona looked at Annie with an expression of complete panic. Annie knew she was thinking that all her hard work to make a perfect meal could be ruined.

Annie stood and patted Connie's shoulder. "Of course. I'll help you upstairs while Leona puts the last touches on her dinner." She looked at Leona and nodded her head toward the kitchen.

"Thank you, dear. Maybe if I rest for a half hour I'll get some strength back."

"Call me when the food is on the table," Chef Marcel

announced as if he was royalty. "I'll be in my room, too." He stomped from the living room with his wine glass in one hand and an almost full wine bottle clenched in the other.

Annie, with one arm under Connie's armpit, helped her to a standing position. Connie kept her other arm curled tightly around Buddy. "Are you sure this is no bother for you?" she asked Annie.

"Don't be silly." What else could she say?

They slowly made their way to the stairs and after what seemed to drag on for the whole night, they finally made it to Connie's room.

"There you go. I'll be back to check on you," Annie said after Connie was stretched out on her bed.

Annie heard snoring before the door was even closed.

4

"My dinner is ruined," Leona sobbed. "I have this perfectly cooked chicken cordon bleu, scalloped potatoes that will get gooey if they sit around any longer, and a beautiful spinach salad for each guest." She picked up a roll from her wicker basket. "These are all cold now. What should I do?"

"Cover your potatoes and keep them warm in the oven. Tent the meat with foil and it will be fine for twenty or thirty minutes. Make some extra sauce for the chicken, which will add some heat when it's served. We can wrap the rolls and reheat them in the oven, too. It's not perfect, but it will work."

Leona nodded and followed Annie's suggestions.

"Besides, by the time everyone is back downstairs, they'll be hungry and won't notice if your meal isn't absolute perfection because it will be close enough."

Leona took a deep breath. Close enough wasn't her standard of perfection. "Okay. I can do this. It's a good thing you made it here tonight or I would be a big pile of mush. I feel like the only one with more anxiety than me is Chef Marcel. I can't help but wonder if he'll still teach his éclair segment tonight or use this storm as an excuse to get out of his commitment."

"That's not *your* problem, Leona. The guests all paid Chef Marcel for the pastry workshop, not you. Besides, I think George will demand it. If he doesn't get his money's worth, he's going to make the chef give him a refund and *that* confrontation won't be pretty," Annie warned.

Annie reached for the tray of condiments for the dining room table when the kitchen was suddenly pitched into darkness. Annie froze, unable to see anything. She waited for her eyes to adjust, but the blackness was a shroud in the kitchen.

Leona gasped. "The power's out?" It was a question with no need for an answer. Her hand wrapped like a vise around Annie's arm. "What? This can't be happening," she moaned.

"You have a generator, don't you?"

"I do but Danny usually takes care of getting it started when the power goes out."

"We'll manage, but the first thing we need is to find some sort of light." Annie pulled open one of the kitchen drawers and felt around with her free hand. Her fingers wrapped around a flashlight. "This should help." She clicked the button. Nothing.

"What'd you find?"

"A flashlight . . . with dead batteries. Where are your candles?"

"On the buffet in the dining room."

Annie carefully felt her way into the dining room. "Oof."

"Be careful of the corner of the table," Leona warned.

"Not helpful after I've already rammed my hip into that corner. Give me a little more notice." Annie tried to keep the annoyance out of her voice, but with a throbbing hip she wasn't very successful.

"Just keep your hands out in front of you and the buffet should be four more steps to your left."

Annie found the buffet, but, unfortunately, her hands also found something else. Whatever it was smashed into a million pieces.

"Oh, no. Don't tell me that was my antique china soup tureen."

"Okay. I won't tell you." Annie's fingers inched over the buffet until she touched what she hoped was one of the hurricane lanterns. They were meant for atmosphere, not emergencies, but were better than nothing. "Where are your matches?"

"In the drawer."

A beam of light illuminated the front of the buffet. Annie turned. "Where'd that light come from?"

Leona had a sheepish grin. "I forgot about the flashlight feature on my cell phone. Can you find the matches now?"

Another beam of light scanned from one side of the room to the other. It gave Annie the creeps, thinking there was an intruder with them in the dining room. "Who's there?"

"It's me. Alex. I thought you might need some help down here." As he spoke, he aimed his beam of light on the buffet and walked toward Annie. "Good. You have candles."

With the help of the light, Annie found the matches and lit all of the candles. "I guess I should check on the guests?" She posed her question to Leona, hoping she would take charge of the situation with a workable plan.

The flickering candles, in a normal situation, would have filled the room with a warm atmosphere, but instead it created moving shapes that were anything but comforting.

"Good idea. I'll try to get the generator started." Leona didn't move.

"I can help you," Alex offered. "That is, if you want some help."

He waited patiently while Annie silently tried to communicate with Leona whether or not she felt safe to go to the garage with this stranger. Leona nodded.

"Okay, then," Annie said. "I'll check on the other guests upstairs and tell them we should have power soon."

"And tell them dinner is ready, too," Leona added. "Before everything is *completely* ruined."

"Got it." Annie carried her hurricane lantern to the stairs. As she paused at the bottom, she felt something brush against her leg. "Is that you, Trouble? Coming with me upstairs?" Annie set the lantern on the bottom step and picked up the kitten. She rubbed her cheek against the soft fur. Trouble vigorously returned the affection, rubbing against Annie's face and purring happily. Company in the darkness, even if it was only Leona's kitten, was better than nothing.

With Trouble nestled in one arm and the lantern providing light, Annie made her way up the stairs. Doors opened and closed and worried voices mixed in the darkness.

"What's happened?" George demanded with Sarah clinging to his arm.

"The power went out but Leona is getting her generator started. No need to panic. We'll be back with lights soon." Annie impressed herself with the confidence in her voice that completely hid the unease she actually felt.

"And what about our dinner?" Sarah asked. "I'm beginning to feel faint." She swiped the back of her hand across her forehead, closed her eyes, and sighed.

Annie clenched her jaw and counted slowly to five. Of course it would be all about someone's stomach at a time like this.

More doors opened and more guests milled around in the hallway.

"Well, if you all want to follow me, I'm sure by the time we're downstairs Leona will have the power on."

Annie held up the lantern to light the stairs and headed down. Shoes tapped on the hardwood and whispers echoed off the walls.

At the bottom, Annie waited while the others caught up with her before she led the way into the dining room which had several hurricane lanterns glowing on the buffet. "I'll be out with the food if you care to seat yourselves."

Annie pushed through into the kitchen just as light flooded the room. She pumped her clenched fist and let out a loud, "Yes."

The back door that led into the mudroom off the kitchen, opened and closed. Annie peeked through the doorway and was relieved to see Leona and Alex. They stomped the snow off their boots and brushed snow off their coats before hanging them on the coatrack.

"Did you get everyone downstairs for dinner?" Leona asked.

"I led the way but I didn't think to do an actual head count." Annie picked up the basket of rolls and the butter. "I'll bring this out and check if everyone made it to the table."

Annie used her hip to push the door to the dining room open and announced, "Here we go. The rest of the meal will be out shortly." Her eyes scanned the table—Sarah, George, Connie with Buddy in her lap, and even Robin sat comfortably at the table. "Where's Chef Marcel? Has anyone seen him since the lights came back on?"

They all glanced at the empty chair and shook their heads. "Maybe he fell asleep," Connie suggested. She helped herself to a roll, breaking off a chunk and giving it to Buddy. "I had a short nap myself but the commotion when the power went out woke me up."

Leona carried in a tray with the chicken cordon bleu and the salad. Alex followed with Leona's casserole of scalloped potatoes. Perfect comfort food for a night like they were having, Annie said to herself.

"Sorry about the power thing." Leona balanced the tray, reached around Connie, and set the platter of meat and the salad on the table.

"No need to apologize," Alex said, adding the scalloped potatoes. "It's not like you could control Mother Nature."

"Yes, well, I still want everyone to have the best experience possible while they're here at the Blackbird."

Robin had a wide grin on her face. "I don't know about anyone else, but I'm having a great time."

She must be enjoying her people watching and analyzing, Annie thought. Her novel, when and if it got written, would be a must read on Annie's TBR list.

"Normally, we serve the guests and leave you to yourselves, but considering the night we're having, Annie and I will eat out here, too," Leona said. "Any objections?"

Connie patted the seat next to hers which was meant for Chef Marcel. "How about you sit right here, Alex?"

Annie added three more placemats on the table and counted out three more sets of silverware from the buffet. Leona placed three snowflake plates on the placemats.

"There." Leona smiled and looked at her guests. "Go ahead and dig into the food. I'm going upstairs to check on Chef Marcel. I'm sure he won't want to miss dinner."

Or that's why he hasn't come down yet, Annie said to herself. It would fit right in with his personality to snub Leona's meal. She glanced at Robin who had her eyes on Alex. That made sense. He was the newcomer and she hadn't had time to analyze him yet. What was her impression of the tall mysterious intruder?

As if Alex sensed that Annie was thinking about him, he turned to her and asked, "What's the story about Chef Marcel?"

"Oh," Connie butted in. "I'll tell you what I know. He travels all over the country teaching pastry making techniques to the novice and experienced. I was so excited when this venue popped up on his Facebook page since it was one I could actually come to now that I'm retired." She lowered her eyes. "I've been a fan of his for quite some time." She reached into her bag that was hooked on the back of her chair. "Here's one of his brochures. He even signed it for me." She beamed with pleasure.

Alex accepted the brochure with a laugh. "Does he pay you to promote him so effectively?"

"Oh, tehe. Now wouldn't that be nice. No, I paid the full price like everyone else."

"Well," Alex said as he looked around the table, "thank you for letting me crash the workshop but don't worry, you won't even know I'm here. And, as soon as the roads are cleared, I'll be on my way."

A loud thump sounded above their heads.

"What was that?" Sarah asked. Her eyes suddenly widened.

"Probably a branch banging against the house," Annie assured her. Her answer didn't reassure herself, though, since the thump was right overhead where one of the guest rooms was. She pushed her chair away from the table. "I'll go upstairs and double check."

"Shouldn't Leona have been back down here by now?" Sarah asked, her voice coming out in barely a whisper.

Annie took the stairs two at a time and almost crashed into Leona on her way down.

"What was that loud thump?"

"I'd better show you." Leona, all color drained from her face, grabbed onto Annie's arm and pulled her down the hall to the first closed door.

With each step, Annie's stomach twisted into a tighter and tighter knot. Whatever was behind the door had spooked Leona. With her hand on the doorknob, Leona looked at Annie. "Ready?"

Annie nodded but her heart said *no*.

The door creaked on its hinges. Leona flipped the light switch. Chef Marcel lay in a heap on the floor.

"Is he—"

Leona nodded before Annie could finish her question.

"Are you sure?"

"I'm no expert, but he sure looks dead to me—he's not

moving, his eyes are staring at nothing. At first I thought he was asleep so I shook him and he rolled off the bed making a big thump. I think it's safe to say that he's dead. And look at this." Leona pointed to a mark around the chef's neck.

Annie felt her jaw drop. "Strangled?"

"I think so. What else would cause that?"

Annie took a quick look around the room, taking in the chef's open suitcase with clothes hanging out, papers spilled near the small desk, and various food items dumped on the dresser.

She turned her attention back to Leona. "So, we're stuck without power . . . the roads are closed . . . and we have a dead man on our hands? What's next?"

The room went dark.

5

M uffled voices filtered up from the dining room below. "The generator went out," Leona said. "At least *that* I can fix . . . I think."

"What do we do with him?" Annie asked in the darkness.

Leona already had her phone out. "I'll call Detective Crank, but whether she can get here or not in this storm is another matter."

Annie felt her way into the hall. A light seeped from under one of the other rooms. "That's odd." She silently walked down the hall, grateful for the oriental runner that absorbed her footsteps. She pressed her ear to the door and listened. Someone was walking around inside but when she'd left the dining room, everyone had been seated around the table. Everyone except Chef Marcel and it definitely wasn't *him* walking around behind this closed door.

A shiver ran through her body. "Leona," Annie called as quietly as possible. She motioned in the dull light for her to hurry closer.

"What?"

Annie pointed to the light.

Leona took four long strides and was at Annie's side with her phone light shining on the door. She grabbed the doorknob and pushed but it was locked. "Is Robin inside? This is the room I put her in," she whispered.

"I don't think so. She was downstairs when I came up after we all heard the thump."

Leona had her master key. "If there's ever a time to use this, I think the time is now. Whoever is in here might be up to some kind of mischief and I've about had all the surprises I can handle today."

By the time Leona got the door unlocked and opened, the room was dark and appeared to be empty. Leona put her arm out to stop Annie from charging inside. She scanned the phone light slowly from side to side. Nothing out of the ordinary caught their attention.

"The bathroom," Annie whispered in Leona's ear.

Before they moved any farther into the room, a voice behind them asked, "Is everything okay up here?"

Both Leona and Annie let out surprised yelps. "I wish you wouldn't keep sneaking up on us, Alex," Annie said. What was it with this guy, anyway? Was he just a super conscientious, helpful guy? Maybe.

"Unless you need help here, I could check the generator before there's complete pandemonium downstairs," he offered. "This crowd can't handle the dark very well. If you want, I'll tell them to sit tight until the lights come back on."

"Yes. Please," Leona said. "We'll be down soon."

"Is everyone still at the table?" Annie asked.

Alex nodded. "Well, except for the chef."

That comment sent another shiver up Annie's spine. Who was in Robin's room?

Alex paused as his eyes scanned around the room. Annie sensed he was making a lightning analysis of the space before he turned and left. Something was odd about his behavior.

As the sound of his footfalls receded down the stairs, Leona approached the bathroom door. Annie picked up one of Robin's boots, thinking it was better than nothing if she needed a weapon.

With one quick movement, Leona slid the bathroom door open and shined her light inside. Still nothing.

"Someone has to be in here somewhere," Annie whispered.

"Maybe it was Trouble. She likes to explore."

"And how do you explain the light? There was light coming from under the door *after* the generator went out."

"Right. I forgot."

Annie pulled the shower curtain to the side. Crouched in the tub, looking at the two women with wide eyes, was a man . . . a young skinny man . . . who looked scared to death. He had a battery powered lantern clutched to his chest.

"Who are you?" demanded Leona.

His mouth opened but nothing came out.

"What are you doing here?" she added without giving him any time to answer the first question.

"I . . . um . . . Robin snuck me in."

"Robin? When?"

"She texted me when everyone was out of the kitchen and she let me in the back door and brought me up here."

"Why?"

The young man rolled his eyes. "Really? We weren't going to waste a paid weekend at this place. Queen bed, great food, no worries about her mother sneaking up on us."

Annie elbowed Leona. "He must be Robin's boyfriend." She lowered the boot she'd been holding. "Get out of the tub. You have to come downstairs with us while we wait for the police to arrive."

"You're having me arrested?" He stood and almost slipped as he lifted one leg over the edge of the tub. "We're sharing the room. Is it because Robin brought food up for me? I only ate the stuff she didn't want."

Annie held his arm. "We'll talk about it later." At this point, until Detective Crank arrived and figured out what had happened to Chef Marcel, it would be easier to share as few details as possible and keep nosey eyes downstairs. "What's your name?"

"Jared."

Light flooded the bathroom as the sound of the generator filled the air. "Geesh, did you have every lightbulb turned on in here?" Leona flipped the switch for the bathroom off. "My electric bill will be through the roof."

"Let's go, Jared. You first," Annie said. She pushed him toward the hall with Leona close behind.

Leona sighed. "That Alex has been a blessing. Good thing his car got stranded nearby. That's about the only thing that has worked out for me tonight."

Alex's arrival was a little *too* convenient, Annie was beginning to think. Or was she being overly suspicious with all the other problems that landed on Leona's doorstep with the storm?

As they made their way down the hall toward the stairs, Jared glanced at Chef Marcel's door. Leona stopped and Annie heard the lock click into place. That was smart. Keep everyone out.

With the lights back on, the fires roaring in the fireplaces, and food on everyone's plates, it almost, but not quite, felt normal.

"Jared?" Robin asked with obvious surprise in her voice.

"Yeah. Busted. Sorry, dude. And now they," Jared jerked his head toward Leona and Annie, "called the police."

"Interesting." Robin helped herself to another scoop of scalloped potatoes.

"You're not gonna defend me? It's not like I broke any law or anything."

"You didn't have to stay here, Jared. I would have been happy to hang out by myself and work on my book after you dropped me off." Robin sipped whatever was in her wine glass.

"You two can sort this out another time," Leona said. "I have called the police and you all might as well know why."

All eyes turned toward Leona.

"It's about Chef Marcel."

"Food poisoning?" George pushed his plate away. "I thought this chicken tasted a little off."

"He didn't eat any chicken," Leona said through clenched teeth.

"Oh, George, Leona's chicken is perfect," Connie said. She turned her attention to Leona. "Maybe you could teach us how to make it if Chef Marcel isn't feeling well?"

"Maybe. We'll see what happens with the storm. My generator isn't big enough to run the whole house. It's powerful enough to keep the lights on, the well pumping water, and the fridge running as long as we have diesel for the generator," Leona explained.

"About that, Leona." Alex scratched the side of his face. "I hate to be the barer of bad news, but I just dumped in the last of the diesel that was stored near the generator. Unless you have more someplace else?"

Would this be the news that pushed Leona over the edge?

She calmly pulled out the chair next to Alex and looked around the table. "I'll gather all my candles and make sure there's plenty of wood for the fireplaces in case this power outage goes on for much longer and we can't keep the generator going."

Sarah whimpered.

Leona gave her a stern look and sat. "Now, I'm going to eat. Jared, take a seat. I don't want this food to go to waste. You too, Annie."

With the chandelier over the table sparkling for the moment, food disappearing, and a semblance of normal chatter around the table, Annie managed to eat Leona's juicy chicken cordon bleu, savory spinach salad, and a small helping of tender scalloped potatoes before the inevitable happened.

"So, Leona, you never did tell us what happened to Chef Marcel. My guess is that he passed out from drinking too much wine. It almost did me in and he had a lot more than I did." Connie dabbed her napkin over her lips. Her fork and knife were perfectly in the center of her spotless plate. Did she let Buddy lick the plate when no one was paying attention? Annie wasn't about to touch that subject.

Leona had a mouthful of chicken so Annie took over the conversation. She'd had some time to remember when everyone had gone upstairs. Any one of the guests could have murdered the chef. "Interesting question, Connie." She looked around the table, stopping to stare at Jared first. "You were hiding in Robin's room. Alex, you went up soon after you arrived." She paused for a sip of wine. "Robin went upstairs next with a plate of food. George and Sarah also went to their room before dinner. I helped Connie upstairs after her fainting spell, and Chef Marcel went upstairs in front of us. It's interesting that all of you were upstairs between the time when he was last seen alive," she paused to look at each guest once more, "and the time he was murdered."

Jared's face turned as white as the snow blowing around outside.

Robin smirked.

George clenched his jaw and turned several shades darker than his wife's pink scarf.

Sarah blinked as if she couldn't even comprehend Annie's words.

Connie swooned dramatically against the back of her chair for the second time since she'd been at the Blackbird.

Buddy licked her face.

Alex was the only one who Annie noticed was watching all the other guests' reactions, just as she was.

"So, which one of you murdered Chef Marcel?" she asked, although she would have been flabbergasted if someone had jumped up and confessed.

6

The dining room was quiet—dead quiet, not-even-anyone-breathing quiet—for several seconds following Annie's question. Mouths fell open and suspicious eyes moved from person to person around the table. A candle sputtered and sizzled. Then everyone reacted at once.

George threw his napkin on the table and pushed himself off his chair. "Well, I'll be expecting two full refunds for this scam of a workshop." He stomped from the room. His shoes clacked on each stair until they were muffled when he reached the oriental runner in the upstairs hallway.

Sarah hustled after George. "Wait, George. I don't think we can get a refund from a dead man."

Jared, his face still white as snow, looked around the table. "Why is everyone staring at *me*? I didn't kill that guy. You believe me, don't you?" His voice squeaked higher with each sentence.

"That's a quick denial for someone who snuck inside and hid upstairs. Or, maybe, your guilty conscience is in panic mode now?" Annie shrugged, dismissing the whole reason for Jared's action as unimportant at the moment. "Whatever. At any rate, it doesn't matter what *we* believe. You'll have your time with Detective Christy Crank when she arrives." An involuntary shudder traveled through Annie at the thought of being in the hot seat under the detective's scrutiny. Christy's intimidating glare. A glare that held the power to melt the coldest snow ball.

"I couldn't have hoped for a more interesting turn of events." Robin grinned and leaned back in her chair. "Coming down for dinner turned out to be a smart decision. This twist just gave me lots of new ideas for my novel."

"What are you talking about?" Connie asked. She had a bit of color back in her cheeks and she reached for a roll. "You sound happy about this horrible event. I can't even begin to figure out what to think about *that*." She turned toward Annie. "Could you be mistaken? It all feels like I've landed in the middle of a dream . . . or nightmare." With another turn of her head, she asked Leona, "What, in heavens name, do we do now?"

"I've called the police department. Detective Crank will be here as soon as possible. But, under the circumstances, I was instructed to lock Chef Marcel's room and keep it off limits to avoid any contamination of the evidence."

"Evidence?" Jared's complexion changed from white to green. His hand covered his mouth and he rushed from the dining room. Footfalls echoed as he charged upstairs.

"What do you think that was all about?" Annie made a point to keep her eyes on Robin. After all, she'd enabled Jared access to the upstairs.

Robin shrugged. "Weak stomach?" She pushed some uneaten potatoes around her empty plate. "How did the chef die? If I was writing something like this in one of my novels, I think I would have poisoned him. Wouldn't that be fitting? French chef dies from eating his own poisoned chocolate éclair."

"How can you joke about this?" Connie snuck a piece of roll to Buddy, putting it on the edge of the table for him. "Besides, we haven't made the éclairs yet." She dabbed a cotton handkerchief under her eyes. "I was so looking forward to having an éclair tonight. Wasn't that what was scheduled?" She looked hopefully at Leona. "Do you have a backup dessert?"

Leona, in the middle of clearing the table was back from the kitchen for another load of dishes. "Well, I'll check. It wasn't part of my responsibility for the weekend. Chef Marcel only ordered meals for the workshop, without desserts," she emphasized.

"I'm sure you can find something, Leona. Check the freezer." Annie picked up the almost empty casserole of scalloped potatoes. "You could offer something that you planned to send to the Black Cat Café."

"I suppose you're right. Business at the café will be slow until the roads are cleared. I'll find something."

Connie clapped her hands. Her concern about Chef Marcel, apparently a distant memory when the current topic of conversation turned to dessert. "What is it?"

Alex took the platter from Leona's hands. "I'll finish this while you share your recipe with Connie."

Annie stacked the rest of the dinner plates and followed Alex into the kitchen. "You don't have to help. You're a guest. I can manage." She thought he was going a bit too far with his Boy Scout pitching-in style. She tried to guide him out of the kitchen but he planted himself in front of the sink and wouldn't budge.

"Technically, I'm not a guest. Helping out is the least I can do after you and Leona so kindly took me in. I get chilled to the bone just thinking that I could be lost under a pile of snow outside, frozen to death." He set the platter in the sink and turned on the water. "Besides, I wanted to talk to you away from Connie. She gets kind of hysterical when anything comes up about the chef."

Annie's attention jumped to high. For someone who'd stumbled to the Blackbird during a storm, she wondered why he had so much interest in that particular guest. "I don't know anything more than what Leona already shared." What information did Alex want? She hadn't meant to sound so defensive but his comment left a bad taste in her mouth. Didn't he realize that everyone in the Blackbird was a potential suspect? Including himself?

"Oh, of course not. What I wanted to tell you is that I think someone went into Chef Marcel's room."

"Oh?"

"Yeah, at some point, maybe thirty or forty-five minutes after I arrived and you showed me to my room, I heard a lot of commotion in the hallway—footsteps, doors opening and closing, that sort of thing."

Annie nodded. "That was around the time that everyone went upstairs to their rooms before dinner."

"At any rate, all the noise caught my attention." He scrubbed the platter in the sink.

Annie waited for him to continue.

Alex chewed on his bottom lip. "I'm curious by nature. I've been going over and over what I heard. It sure sounded like the chef's door opened and closed several times which makes me assume that someone went in."

"You could hear his door?"

"Remember, the room you so kindly let me use is next to the chef's."

Annie picked up a drying towel. "Did you see *who* went in?" She stacked the clean pots and pans in the cupboard.

"No, just the door clicking. I counted, there were three times the door clicked open then closed. I don't know what it all means but it's just that, you know, in light of what has happened, I thought it might be a relevant bit of information."

"When Detective Christy Crank gets here you can tell her. I'm sure she'll want to interview everyone." For all Annie knew, the chef might have opened and closed his door for some reason. Or, and this concerned her the most, Alex made it all up to throw suspicion away from himself.

Annie heard scratching on the kitchen door from the dining room side. She pushed it open. "Well, hello Buddy." Seeing the adorable dachshund made her even more homesick for her cozy living room with the fireplace, Jason, and her own dog and cats.

Buddy made a beeline to the back door.

"I guess you need to go outside?" Annie asked the dachshund. "Let me check with Connie first. I don't want to do something that could upset her even more than she already is."

Annie poked her head into the dining room. "Do you mind if I take Buddy out? I could use a bit of fresh air myself."

"You don't mind? I'm sure he won't go far with those short legs and all the snow out there. Let me put his sweater on."

Leona used that interruption to pile the last of the dirty dishes and bring them into the kitchen. She rolled her eyes as she walked by Annie. "A sweater?"

Alex snorted but continued scrubbing pots at the sink.

After Connie retrieved Buddy's red and black plaid sweater along with four little booties and his blue leash, she helped herself to coffee.

"That's not hot anymore," Leona said.

Connie waved her free hand. "No worries. At this point, anything that can give me a little kick is perfect. Did you find any dessert yet?"

"Not yet. How about you check the fire in the living room? Add a couple logs so we have one toasty room while I finish up in here and Annie takes Buddy outside." Leona tied her apron around her waist. "Just a couple of logs, we don't want the living room to turn into a furnace again."

"I'll check the diesel situation in the generator for you to see if it needs more yet." Alex dried his hands, waiting for a response.

"You don't mind?" Leona asked. "I guess I have to scrounge up some sort of dessert or I'll never hear the end of it."

"Glad to help after you more or less saved my life." Alex headed toward the front door where his boots and other warm clothes had been left.

Annie followed. She bundled up and opened the door for

42 LYNDSEY COLE

Buddy, stuffing his leash in her pocket. With the snow, Buddy wasn't going to be going far. He hesitated before plunging off the step and almost disappearing into a snow drift. With a couple of leaps and bounds, he found a spot near a bush where the wind had blown most of the snow away and he lifted his leg.

Annie used the shovel to clear off the top step. Snow still swirled around her but it wasn't blinding and the trees swayed gently.

"I think the storm is winding down," Alex hollered from further along the path. He left boot prints on the path which made it easy for Annie to see where she needed to shovel.

The driveway, buried under more drifts of snow, was a white desert with only car tops showing through. But the road beyond had one lane cleared and the lone streetlight shone brightly.

"Hey," Annie shouted. "The power must be back on."

While Annie pushed her shovel through the deep snow, Buddy followed closely behind.

Alex tromped to the garage and disappeared inside. With the generator suddenly silenced, the quiet that blanketed Annie brought a temporary but welcome calm. Without the background noise, she forced her brain to focus on the mess inside the Blackbird.

"I'll go in and help Leona unless you want me to do some shoveling," Alex said on his way back to the house.

"I need the exercise. Tell Leona I'll be in shortly. Buddy is having too much fun out here." Annie had to admit that having Alex get stranded at the Blackbird did have some benefits with all the help he provided. He was one of the brighter spots, or possibly the *only* bright spot, of the evening except for the nagging suspicion that there was more to him than he had revealed.

"Maybe Buddy's happy to be out of Connie's clutches for ten minutes." They both watched as Buddy leaped through the snow, disappearing for a second before reappearing nose-first and then diving in again. "Don't strain your back with all that shoveling," Alex said before he disappeared inside.

Alone in the dark, Annie had time to think while she shoveled toward the cars. The chef had annoyed everyone in the short time they'd all been together at the Blackbird and any one of the guests could have slipped into his room unnoticed. But who?

With the last shovelful of snow thrown off the walkway, Annie leaned on her shovel and waited for her breathing to return to normal. Randy, Leona's neighbor, swung into the driveway with his big plow truck, followed by a black Dodge Charger. After Randy cleared what he could, Detective Christy Crank pulled her Dodge Charger forward and shut the engine off.

Annie waited with mixed emotions. Detective Crank stepped from her car.

"Nice evening for a murder," Christy said. Her knitted hat was pulled low over her forehead ending just above her dark rimmed glasses. She pushed her glasses up on her nose. Her heavy winter boots squeaked as she walked on the cold snow. "How many people are inside?"

"Seven. Leona and six guests. And one body," she added.

Buddy charged at Christy and barked at her ankles.

"This sounds like a feisty one." Christy kneeled on one knee and let the dachshund sniff her glove. That's all it took for Buddy to leap at Christy's face and lick her from chin to glasses.

Christy threw her head back. "Eww. I never kiss on the first date."

Annie couldn't help but chuckle. Detective Christy Crank had a soft spot for animals even while she held a hard line with their two-legged humans.

7

"Give me a little information on what I'll be dealing with inside." Detective Crank folded her arms as she stood with Annie on the narrow path leading to the Blackbird's front door. Her stance screamed business but she couldn't take her eyes off the small dog's antics.

In stark contrast, the lights along the path leading to the front door, which suddenly broke through the darkness, sparkled warmly and gave no hint of the tragedy inside.

"Don't you think your first impression, not clouded by my comments, is important?" Annie was far too familiar with Christy's method of twisting her statements to sound like something other than what Annie had meant. She refused to end up in Christy's web.

"What I think is that you need to answer my questions, Ms. Hunter. Did you forget why I'm here?"

Annie crossed her arms, mirroring Christy's aggressive stance. "Of course I haven't forgotten."

"I met the dog. What about the six guests? Male? Female? Do you have a *gut* feeling about any of them?"

Annie bristled at the mention of a gut feeling. She did, and

Detective Crank managed to ridicule it every time. "Do you mean do I have information as to who killed the chef? If that's your question then, no, I have no information."

Christy dropped her arms. "Clever answer. We'll leave it at that. For now." With no further attempts at uncovering information, she trudged up the narrow path to the door and followed Buddy inside.

Annie sucked in a big lungful of cold air. She needed this quiet moment for calm reflection while her brain swirled with possibilities of what could be a motive behind killing Chef Marcel—anger, theft, an unfortunate accident? He certainly didn't endear himself to his workshop participants, which was odd in itself for someone who relied on his reputation to further his business.

Before her thoughts traveled any further, an SUV turned into the Blackbird's driveway. A load of worry fell away from Annie. She should have known Jason would come as soon as the roads were cleared but with so much going on, she'd forgotten to even update him on the events.

Her smile was greeted first by her terrier mix, Roxy, who bounded from the car and danced around Annie's legs. Her limitless energy and affection marked by several woofs lifted Annie's spirit. By the time Jason reached her side and wrapped her in his strong arms, Roxy had moved on to sniffing around all the smells Buddy left on the path.

"We couldn't wait for a phone call to find out how everything was going here. Wondering and waiting made these last few hours drag like I was walking through a pot of Leona's fudge. And, speaking of Leona, is she managing everything with her usual organized chaos?"

"I don't even know where to begin," Annie said. "If time dragged for you, it leaped along like a cheetah chasing its dinner around here. Did you notice who else is parked here?"

Jason looked at the cars behind them. "Detective Crank? What's that about?"

"I guess the grape vine in town was off along with the power." Annie put her arm through Jason's and they walked slowly toward the house. "Before we go inside, I'll give you the short version. Leona had the pastry workshop this weekend with Chef Marcel."

"Yeah. She explained that when she called to tell me you were coming here to help."

"Well, he was murdered . . . in his room. Christy told Leona to lock the room until she could get here."

Jason stopped walking. "You're kidding, right?"

"I wish." Annie shook her head and let out a deep sigh. "In hindsight, I wish I never answered Leona's phone call and went straight home to enjoy being snowed in with you. This has been a horrible few hours."

Jason hugged Annie again. "I would have preferred that too, but I'm glad you were here to help Leona. You're her rock when things start to crumble. You know that, right?"

"Of course I do, but still. If my phone had been in my coat pocket and I didn't hear it ring—"

"You'd be feeling terribly guilty when you saw the missed call."

Annie tilted her head and looked into Jason's eyes. "You know what Leona said to me when I told her to call you about my change of plans?"

Jason grinned. "She'd never cook for me again if I didn't say yes?"

"Well, she might have thought of that later. No, she said, 'He'll understand.' Thanks for that. I guess." Annie put her cheek against Jason's chest and said a silent thank you for having him in her life. "How about we make a mad dash for the car and escape to our cozy house away from this craziness?"

Jason kissed the top of Annie's head. "As wonderful as that

sounds, I'm afraid it's too late for any kind of escape. Unless, of course, you don't care that Leona just opened the door and is waving frantically for us to come inside. Roxy already accepted the invitation. What do you think? Abandon Roxy and run to my car or head inside and help to dilute the situation?"

"Annie! Jason!" Leona's voice boomed through the air. "What are you waiting for? Detective Crank is eating leftovers while all the guests pace around in the living room waiting for her to question them. I'm afraid there could be another murder."

Annie and Jason exchanged a look that said they both hoped this was just Leona being overly dramatic but they did hustle inside.

"Is this Christy's strategy to make all the suspects sweat?" Annie asked as she shrugged out of her parka and slid her feet out of her boots.

"I don't know. She said she was hungry. Can you talk to her? George threatened to leave. Connie is swooning every five minutes. Robin keeps tapping away on her phone. I don't know where Jared went."

"What about Alex? He's been more than helpful but there's something about him that makes me suspicious," Annie whispered.

"Alex? He's the only sane one here, if you want my opinion. Me included." Leona ran her fingers through her hair. "Should I make coffee and offer dessert as if there's nothing wrong?"

Jason gave Leona a quick hug. "Calm down. Christy's just in her make-'em-sweat-till-they-squeal mode. I'd love coffee and dessert even if everyone else has lost their appetite."

"He's right, Leona." Annie put her arm around her aunt's waist. "What did you find for dessert anyway? I'm sure that will bring Connie back to life."

"Well, I've been saving this for a special occasion. It's a pecan pie cheesecake. There are probably five hundred calories in one bite and I'm dying to see how it came out."

Annie chuckled. Getting Leona to talk about food got her mind off of murder quicker than melting a snowball in front of the fire. "I'll get out the plates and forks, Jason can check on the fire, and you can get the coffee going."

A blur of white terrier and brown dachshund streamed by Annie's legs, almost tripping her as she turned toward the dining room table to find plates for dessert. At least the dogs were enjoying themselves. It must be nice to be so unaffected by the tension at the Blackbird.

"Leona said she's getting a pot of coffee ready." Detective Crank, sitting alone at the big table, set her fork down on a well-cleaned plate of leftovers. Her comment sounded innocent enough but her words scratched down Annie's spine like nails on a chalkboard. There was always something behind her words.

"Yes. And she's sharing one of her latest desserts." Annie returned to the buffet for one more plate. Christy had a sweet tooth a mile long and was sure to want a piece of the creamy cheesecake with her coffee.

"Perfect. That will give us a chance for a friendly chat before I get to the, ah . . ."

"Suspects?" Annie raised one eyebrow as she directed her question Christy's way.

"Well, that's exactly why I want to talk to you. Your insight about each guest could prove to be helpful." Christy pushed her plate away, leaned back in her chair, and sighed satisfactorily. Annie doubted that Christy cared at all what she thought and was tempted to drop a fork on her head as she walked by, but forced her hand to hold the silverware tightly.

"How about you bring back coffee and dessert for the two of us while Leona serves her guests in the living room. I'm sure they won't mind having a snack before I chat with them."

"A chat? Is that what you call interrogating witnesses?"

"Whatever puts them at ease." Christy flicked her fingers toward the kitchen. "Coffee?"

Annie slammed through the door into the kitchen. How dare Christy order her around like a servant? Leona had the coffee pot, cups, sugar, and cream on a tray. Another tray held two-inch slices of cheesecake.

"Did Christy even go upstairs into Chef Marcel's' room when she got her?" Annie found a smaller tray and added two cups of coffee along with two plates of the pecan pie cheesecake.

"Christy confirmed what I already told her and put crime tape over the door. She said she has to wait for the forensic team to arrive. They're on their way. Apparently, the storm caused a big delay for the rest of the team." Leona rolled her eyes. "Great for me. Now I've got a mutinous bunch of guests to try to placate."

As Annie picked up the tray, her thumb slipped and jammed into one piece of cheesecake. She set the tray down and licked the cheesecake off before jamming it in again. "Oh, this is heavenly, Leona." She made a mental note to give that piece to Christy. "I might need seconds."

"You tasted it already?"

"Just the bit of Christy's cheesecake that ended up on my thumb."

Leona looked at Annie. She snorted before they both burst out laughing. "I'm sure you won't tell her *that*."

The door swung open. Both Leona and Annie spun around to see who it was. "Thank goodness it's only you, Jason." Annie's hand hovered over her chest. "If Christy caught us talking about her, we'd be sent in to sweat with the suspects."

"I could hear the two of you yukking it up in here. You're lucky though, since Christy's on her phone and she was probably too distracted to hear you. What's going on?"

Annie picked up the tray. "I'd better deliver this to her highness before she does come in here looking for her coffee and dessert." She turned around, using her backside to push through the door to the dining room.

"It's about time. Were you waiting for Leona to finish baking?" Christy set her phone on the table.

"The coffee wasn't quite ready," Annie lied. She put the tray on the table. One cup of coffee and a piece of cheesecake was set in front of Christy. Annie took her piece and stood near the window. "You'd better eat fast, it sounds like the rest of your team just pulled in." Annie hoped this bit of news would get her off the hook with having to chat with Christy.

"Go let them in. That will give me enough time to enjoy this creamy sweetness. You and I can chat later."

Annie smiled to herself at her lucky break before she shoved a big forkful of pecan pie cheesecake into her mouth and watched as Christy scooped from the spot where Annie's finger had been. She managed to keep from laughing until she was out of the room and headed toward the front door.

Annie bumped into George, suitcase in hand. "Making an escape?" she asked.

"I can't stand to be here for one more minute while that detective makes us sit and wait while she does who knows what." He set his suitcase down and reached for his coat. "Sarah better hurry up or I'll leave her here."

Annie watched with amusement. Obviously, George had no clue that even if Christy allowed anyone to leave, all the cars were blocked in by at least half a dozen vehicles. She opened the door to the new arrivals. "Right this way." She held her arm out. "You'll figure it out once you get to the top of the stairs."

After the trail of men, women, and equipment disappeared upstairs, George scowled. "Someone needs to move those vehicles so I can get out."

"Well, tell that to Detective Crank. She's standing right behind you," Annie said to George.

"Running off already?" Detective Crank stood with her hands on her hips, staring at George as he huffed and puffed his frustration. "Didn't I tell all of you to sit tight?" She stepped right up close to George. "What's the hurry?"

"I, uh, you can't keep me here."

Christy's eyebrows raised so high it made her glasses slide to the end of her nose. "Now that's where you're wrong, George. It is George, isn't it?"

George nodded.

Sarah, with her suitcase bumping behind her on each and every stair, stopped at the bottom. "Oh, hello Detective Crank. George told me you said we could leave."

Annie moved back a couple of steps but she wasn't going to miss this show.

"Oh really?" Christy said. "I'm not sure where he got that idea from but since I'm such a nice person, I'll give you three minutes to put your suitcases over by the stairs and get yourselves into the living room before I decide to question you at the station instead." She looked at her watch. "You've already wasted half a minute."

George shoved his suitcase next to Sarah's and pushed them both out of the way. He grabbed Sarah's arm and they disappeared.

Christy paused next to the suitcases. "I can't wait to get a look inside these matching leather suitcases. They certainly spent a pretty penny on them." She turned to look at Annie. "Why do you suppose George was so anxious to get out of here?"

Annie stared at the suitcases. Wasn't that only *one* of the million-dollar questions settling at the Blackbird Bed and Breakfast after Chef Marcel's sudden murder?

8

A fter arriving home late the night before, Annie tossed and turned before she finally fell asleep. Waking up in her own bed Saturday morning had been an unexpected surprise after the snowstorm, power outage, and murder at Leona's bed and breakfast the night before. A shudder passed through her body with the memory. She slowly uncurled her legs and let her feet inch into the cold corner of her sheets.

Roxy jumped on the bed and licked Annie's cheek. "Really? You can't let me have two minutes to actually wake up completely?" She laughed and pulled the down comforter over her head.

Roxy whined.

"Okay. You win. I hope coffee is ready when I get downstairs."

As if she understood, Roxy jumped off the bed and her nails clicked on each step as she descended. "Ha. Has she learned how to operate the coffee machine now?"

"No. But you know that's one of *my* specialties," Jason said from the doorway. "Roxy and I are a tag team—her job is to get you out of bed after I tell her the coffee is ready."

Annie's nose crinkled. "Ah. The rich aroma is *almost* enough to give me the jolt I'll need today." She let her toes dance on the floor until they slid into her sheepskin lined scuffs. With a fleece over her PJs, she followed Jason downstairs.

"A crackling fire, hot coffee, and," she walked to the door leading to the porch on the lake side of the house, "what appears to be the beginning of a clear day; what more could I ask for?"

Jason slid a plate next to her mug of coffee.

"What's this?" Annie touched the pastry that surrounded something.

"A pastry-wrapped, caramel-stuffed baked apple."

Annie puffed her lips out and gave Jason a skeptical look. "From where?"

"What? You don't think I can ever manage to make anything delicious?" Jason busied himself with wiping an already clean counter instead of meeting Annie's eyes.

"Jason? You are also the worst liar in all of Catfish Cove." She carefully pushed her fork into the puff pastry and a thick gooey caramel filling oozed out. She felt her mouth water with anticipation.

"It's something new Leona is working on. She thought it might impress Chef Marcel when she served something elegant like this for breakfast during the workshop."

"Ha! Nothing would impress that man unless it was a creation of his own and he could claim credit for it."

Now it was Jason's turn to look shocked. "You were barely there long enough to have a decent chat with the man."

"True, but with a personality as, um, wretched as his, it only took a short amount of time for his true colors to shine . . . with a dark glow. He criticized Leona every chance he got, turning her into a Nervous Nellie." Annie blew on the steaming apple and speared a portion with her fork.

"Don't stick that in your mouth yet unless you want a burned tongue," Jason warned.

Annie let the sweet, tart treat hover in front of her mouth as the caramel dripped from her fork into a long stalactite. She tested the temperature with the tip of her tongue before deciding it was okay to pop the piece in her mouth. Her eyes rolled up as she savored the perfect blend of the tart apples, buttery pastry, and sweet caramel. "This is sinfully delicious. Where did Leona get this idea from?"

"You won't believe me if I tell you."

Annie felt her forehead wrinkle. You gave her the idea?"

"Uh-huh." Jason sipped his coffee, barely concealing the grin on his face. "I ordered something like this the last time I went to an out-of-the-way coffee shop in Boston. It wasn't half as good as Leona's creation, though. I think she found a new specialty for the Black Cat Café."

Annie nodded enthusiastically. "This would work for breakfast, lunch, or dessert with the appropriate side. Maybe yogurt and granola as a breakfast; extra apples and cheddar cheese for a lunch; vanilla ice cream for a dessert."

"I suppose you could promote it as a healthy choice if you emphasize that it's mostly fruit."

"Right. How do I explain away all the sugar in the caramel and the fat in the pastry though?" Annie got down to business devouring the rest of her pastry-wrapped, caramel-stuffed apple.

"I forgot to tell you last night with all the craziness at the Blackbird, but Thelma called yesterday afternoon to make sure you got home safely." Jason sat next to Annie.

"Oh. Was she ok? I don't suppose her son could make it over to help her when the power went out." Annie's elderly neighbor, who lived alone just a few houses down from Jason and Annie, would never want anyone to battle through the snow to help her if it meant putting that person in danger.

"Roxy and I checked on her. She put up a big fuss when we got to her house but it was also clear that she was relieved to see us. Her gas fireplace managed to keep her living room warm enough and she had a couple extra blankets over her legs."

"And Moby?"

Jason laughed. "That big Maine Coon cat was curled up on her lap and probably gave off more heat than an electric blanket."

"Thank you for checking up on her. I can't believe she worried about *me* during the storm." Annie finished her coffee and held her cup toward Jason. "Any more coffee? I could use another half a cup before I head off to work."

"Of course she worries about you. You and Roxy visit her more than her own son does. She asked me to tell you that she looks forward to a visit from you as soon as you have time to stop by." Jason walked to the coffee machine and filled Annie's cup.

Annie laughed. "She must be out of sweets. I'll bring her one of these caramel apple thingies and she'll probably write me into her will."

"No wonder her son isn't fond of you. He worries that you're his competition."

"To be honest, in my opinion, he should do more but I'm happy to fill the gap. She's such a caring and thoughtful woman. And she knows everyone who has lived in town for any length of time. Roxy and I will swing by this afternoon." Annie slid off the stool. "But now I'd better get dressed and get my butt over to the café just in case there's any business today."

Annie ran upstairs, found a clean pair of jeans and a turtle-neck, brushed her mass of strawberry blonde curls, and slipped her favorite sweater on. She pulled her silver snowflake necklace to the outside and headed back downstairs. As she pushed her feet into her boots, her phone rang. A quick glance made her stomach twist. "I'm not sure I want to answer this call from Leona," Annie said to Jason. "What if there was another disaster last night after we left?"

"We would have already heard. You may as well answer because she won't stop calling."

"Hello." Annie balanced the phone between her shoulder and cheek and half-listened to several minutes of Leona's story as she gathered her hat, gloves, and scarf in a pile on the dining room table next to her shoulder bag.

"Okay." Annie dropped her phone into her bag.

"That was quick. At least on your end."

"Leona is sending the workshop attendees to the Black Cat Café for breakfast and a change of scenery. Well, she actually said she needed to get them out of the Blackbird before she strangled someone. No one is allowed to leave town, per order of Detective Crank. With Chef Marcel dead, the workshop is cancelled and they're all sniping at each other."

"Sounds—"

"Awful?"

"Actually, I was thinking more along the lines that everyone is suspicious of the rest of the group and wondering who is the killer in their midst. Who is your best guess?"

Annie leaned against the table. "First, I just want to say I'm so happy I didn't have to spend the night at the Blackbird. With Danny getting home to help Leona, I was okay leaving all that mayhem far behind once Christy was done with me." Annie couldn't keep the disdain out of her voice when she uttered the detective's name.

"Yeah, I already figured *that* out."

"As to your question? Chef Marcel annoyed everyone."

"Everyone?" Jason looked shocked.

"Yes. In the short time I was around him . . . remember George? He tried to sneak out before Detective Crank questioned him?"

Jason nodded.

"George was already pushing for a refund before dinner last night. His wife, Sarah, goes along with whatever George says."

"So two refunds? That's a hit in the chef's pocketbook."

"Exactly. And then Robin, a local and the youngest person at the workshop, told me that she doesn't even like baking. She came because her mother gave her the workshop as a gift and she was enjoying studying everyone for her novel."

Jason's eyebrows rose halfway to his hairline.

"Plus, she snuck her boyfriend, Jared, in and he was upstairs until we discovered him hiding in the tub in her room *after* the chef was murdered." Annie emptied her jeans pocket into her bag, throwing in her lip balm and some loose change.

"So, you're thinking *he* might have done the annoying chef in? But what would be his motive?"

"Good question, which I have no answer for yet. But if Jared *is* the murderer, I think he's too dumb, careless, or both to have gotten rid of all evidence that he was in the chef's room." She wrapped her scarf around her neck.

Jason carried the empty plate and coffee cups to the sink. "What about the other guests?"

Annie scrunched her lips to one side. "Connie, with her dog Buddy, hovered around like she was the hostess. She seemed to be the only one who was actually enjoying herself. Of course, as soon as anything happened, she covered her forehead and had a swooning episode," Annie raised her own arm to her head, closed her eyes, and pretended to go weak in her legs, "but she managed to recover in a heartbeat as soon as food was mentioned."

Jason chuckled. "Food, the quickest cure for a fainting female. Does that have a catchy ring or what?"

Annie shook her head in response.

"Any other guests?"

"One more—Alex." Annie reached for the door but stopped and turned back toward Jason. "He wasn't supposed to be at the Blackbird but he showed up after his car got stuck in the snow."

"Huh. Your expression is telling me you aren't convinced about his story." Jason leaned on the counter, one leg crossed in front of the other.

"He was the only one who never fell apart when everything got crazy. He stayed calm and helped Leona with the generator."

Annie shrugged. "Maybe he's just that kind of guy—like you—helpful, good in stressful situations, but—"

"But something doesn't add up. Is that what you're thinking?" Jason asked.

"With the chef dead, all the guests have to be looked at from a different perspective. Fortunately, that's Detective Crank's job and not mine." Annie turned the doorknob.

"Good to hear that you won't be sticking your nose in this mess."

With the door open, Annie ignored Jason's jab. "You can take Roxy out for her morning walk? I really need to rush to the café now that I know we'll have breakfast customers who need to be treated with kid gloves."

"Yes. Roxy and I will enjoy a peaceful walk along the Lake Trail after the sun has warmed the path."

Annie glared. "That's so not fair."

"Good luck." Jason blew a kiss.

Annie hustled to her car, dusted the snow off the windshield, and climbed inside. She turned on her radio, hoping it would keep her from thinking too much about all the possibilities for something to go wrong while Leona's guests ate breakfast at the Black Cat Café.

9

The parking lot behind the building that housed the Black Cat Café was plowed clear with only two cars parked already—Greta's and Mia's. Even though Annie technically ran the café now that Leona and Danny had the Blackbird Bed and Breakfast to manage, her manager, Greta, and her mother usually beat her to the café in the mornings.

"Well, at least there's plenty of help this morning," Annie said to herself. "Plenty of reliable and competent help." She walked to the front of the building along the shoveled path, squinting as the rising sun sparkled on the new snow with blinding intensity.

When Annie pushed the door open and walked into the Black Cat Café, soft piano music met her ears. The aroma of freshly brewed coffee and steaming hot blueberry muffins filled her nose.

An apron came flying through the air. Annie's hand shot out and caught it, a motion that had become second nature to her. "We've got Leona's guests coming in for breakfast," Annie's mother said. "And, yes, Greta made new aprons. What do you think?"

Annie looked at the black cats surrounded by dark blue

snowflakes on a crisp white background and nodded. "Very appropriate for the weather we've been having." She tied the apron around her waist. "Greta, did Leona tell you about her latest culinary creation?"

"Well, if you're referring to her pastry-wrapped, caramel-filled apple, then, yes, we discussed it during one of Leona's daily calls to make sure I haven't changed my mind about this job." Greta snickered. "I don't tell her I love it since I want to keep her on her toes. Even though her focus is on the Blackbird Bed and Breakfast, she still owns the Black Cat Café and she needs to stay involved. Is that mean of me to look at it that way?"

"Not at all," Annie said.

"Besides," Mia added, "I know my sister and she'll never back off from being on top of what's going on at this place. The bed and breakfast is Danny's dream but, Leona's heart will always be at the Black Cat Café." Her eyes searched the counters. "Where are these new apple pastries? I still have room to fill up one of the trays in the pastry display for them."

"I don't have that many yet. Plus, don't tell Leona, but I tweaked her recipe a little."

Both Annie and Mia burst out laughing at Greta's admission.

"Oh boy," Annie said. "Leona won't like it if yours are tastier."

Greta pulled a dish towel off a tray revealing twelve perfectly browned pastry-covered apples. Steam rose from the apples. "I made half the way she said but I added some crystallized ginger to the rest. It's not a big change, just a bit of a zip for those who like ginger." She cut one of the apples into quarters. Rich caramel oozed from the center. Greta made sure that a piece of ginger adorned each slice before she gave a sample to Annie and Mia.

Annie quickly poured herself some coffee and sat at the counter in front of one of the plates. With her fork, she cut a big chunk of the apple with plenty of pastry, caramel, and the chunk of ginger. "My mouth is watering." She didn't bother to tell the other women that she'd already sampled one of Leona's masterpieces with Jason. She didn't want Greta to think she was comparing the two cooks' baking skills. She savored the treat. It was excellent.

Mia was first to exhale a long, satisfied sigh. Her eyes closed and her body sagged. With her mouth full of apple and caramel, she mumbled, "Exquisite." After she swallowed, she added, "I love the pop of ginger but I know it's not everyone's thing." She turned to Annie. "No comment?"

Annie gave a thumbs-up sign and pointed to her mouth which was filled with the tart and sweet gooeyness of Greta's creation. Once she could talk without having anything dribble from her mouth, she replied, "These will be a hit, but I do think they are best warm."

Greta and Mia nodded their agreement.

"What do you think about serving the apples with granola and yogurt for breakfast, cheddar cheese for lunch, and ice cream for a dessert?" Annie wanted a second opinion on her earlier idea.

"Perfect," Greta said. "Leona already thought of that very breakfast idea for this morning for when her guests arrive. The whole menu for them will be the pastry-wrapped apples with a cheese and egg croissant along with their choice of beverage."

Annie glanced at the big clock over the entrance to the café and hopped up from her counter stool. "Enough of all this eating and chatting. Guests will be arriving soon and they always make a beeline to the beverage cart first."

Mia moved to the pastry display and continued to fill the trays with muffins, scones, sweet breads, and cookies. The timer for the oven beeped and another tray of delicious aromas filled the café when Greta pulled out a tray of individual fruit pies.

As Annie busied herself making a fresh pot of coffee for customers, checking the supply of tea offerings, and topping off the sugar and cream containers, the café door squeaked. It's too early, she thought before she turned around to face Detective Crank walking in alongside the Chief of Police, Tyler Johnson.

Annie's heart skipped a beat. Even though she was long over her relationship with Tyler, he still triggered old and fond memories especially since she hadn't bumped into him for so long.

"Is the coffee hot yet?" Christy asked. She walked to the drink cart and helped herself to a mug. "We thought we'd come a little early to beat the crowd."

And have a chance to annoy us, Annie said to herself. But she pasted a smile on to hide her true feelings about Detective Crank. "A few more minutes for this new pot of coffee but the water is hot for tea if you can't wait."

"I'll wait." She headed to the pastry display and bent down to get a closer look.

Tyler put a tea bag in his travel mug.

"Tea?" Annie said. "I don't remember you for a tea drinker, Tyler."

"Actually, my new friend converted me. Well, not completely, but it's a way for me to cut back on coffee but still enjoy a hot drink." Tyler became fascinated with trying to brush an imaginary piece of lint off his sleeve when he mentioned his 'new friend.'

She noticed a slight tint of pink creep into his cheeks. In a low voice, she said, "That's great . . . about your new friend." She threw away his used tea bag. "Anyone I know?"

"Tyler," Christy called, "I've got you an egg croissant. Do you want anything else before we head back to the Blackbird?"

"Gotta go, Annie." He screwed the top on his travel mug and joined Christy.

His relief at the interruption softened his face which only made Annie more curious who the mysterious 'friend' was. That secret wouldn't stay hidden for long. Not that it was any of her business, but she hoped it was someone she approved of. Even if Tyler didn't know it yet, Annie did hope for the best for him.

Tyler left the café but Christy wandered over to where Annie was still standing by the drink cart. "I never got a chance to ask you what rooms you went into last night at the Blackbird." She tucked her breakfast bag under her arm and filled her travel mug with the now steaming fresh coffee.

"What do you mean?"

"Simple question, Annie. What rooms did you go into after you arrived and before the victim was discovered?"

"The victim. You mean Chef Marcel?"

Christy rolled her eyes. "Of course that's who I mean. Quit stalling and answer my question. It's not difficult."

"I helped Connie to her room after she got overheated and fainted. And after Leona went up to investigate the loud thump, I went up to Chef Marcel's room."

"And Leona was in there when you arrived?"

"No, I met her on the stairs and we went in together. The chef was on the floor. That was the loud noise we all heard."

"Was that noise before or after Leona went upstairs?"

"Leona went upstairs to see if the Chef wanted to come down for dinner. There was a thump. I went up. He was on the floor."

Christy sipped her coffee. "Who else went into his room?"

Annie leaned right into Christy's face. "If I knew the answer to that, I'd probably know who the murderer was," Annie hissed. "Isn't that *your* job to find the clues that the killer left behind?"

Christy smiled. "I just wanted to know why we found yours and Leona's fingerprints in the chef's room."

"No one else's?"

"Well, now, I can't reveal that tidbit, can I?" Christy held up the coffee and breakfast bag. "Thanks. I always love my visits here." With that comment, she turned and walked out.

Annie stood in her spot and steamed. That whole conversation gave Annie no new information but she suspected that Christy had fun watching her twist and spin under the scrutiny.

Before she could dissect the exchange any more, the café door opened for business.

Connie strutted in with her shoulders back and her purse dangling from her elbow as she approached Annie. "What a cute little spot. Now I see why Leona suggested we all come here for breakfast." She cupped her hand around her mouth and spoke close to Annie's ear. "I had to get out of that place before it suffocated me with that shroud of death."

10

———

Connie barely touched Annie's arm before she pointed to a booth with a view of Heron Lake. "I'll make myself comfy over there. Could you bring me a large coffee, please? With a big shot of half and half, no sugar." She waved to Sarah who'd just walked in. Alone. "Come sit with me, hon, Annie's bringing coffee."

Annie swallowed the words she wanted to say to Connie— something along the lines of *please,* help yourself. *But,* since these were Leona's bed and breakfast guests she bit her tongue, assuming they probably had the expectation of being served. She relaxed her clenched jaw and fixed two coffees, both the same. Sarah could walk to the drink cart to adjust hers if necessary.

This was going to be a long morning.

". . . and then I heard someone say it looked like strangulation," Annie overheard Connie whisper to Sarah as she set the coffees on the table. Connie plumped her gray curls. "He didn't know I was standing in the doorway leading to the foyer."

Sarah's face turned from a pink blush from the cold outside air to white that matched the snow. "Strangled? How gruesome." She twisted the napkin in her hands to a tight knot then shredded it into tiny bits of paper that landed in a pile in front of her.

"You heard Detective Crank say that?" Annie asked.

"No, it definitely wasn't her since what I heard was a male's voice." Connie clearly was thrilled to be the center of attention while delivering this juicy tidbit.

The police chief possibly? Annie wondered.

Connie shrugged. "No one noticed me with all the people going up and down the stairs, in and out letting cold air inside, and tromping snow on those beautiful floors." Connie shook her head. "Leona will have to do some refinishing after the mess left behind from all those feet." She folded her hands. "What's on the menu for breakfast?"

By now, all the Blackbird Bed and Breakfast guests were sitting around the café. George pouted by himself at a small table near the French doors. Why wasn't he sitting with his wife over here with Connie? Annie wondered. Robin and Jared were at another booth. Robin sat tall and straight with her eyes glued to her phone as she tap-tapped away. Jared slumped over the table with his head resting on his arms. Alex sat at the counter nursing a cup of coffee while he chatted with Greta.

A few more early customers were scattered around the café with hot drinks and sweet confections. They chattered about the storm and seemed to be enjoying the cozy atmosphere. It looked like any other morning but with the chef's murder hanging in the air, Annie knew that looks were deceiving.

"So? Breakfast?" Connie's question brought Annie back to the task at hand. "I don't want to dawdle for too long since I had to leave Buddy at the Blackbird. Leona assured me she would keep an eye on him but he gets terrible anxiety when he's separated from me."

"No worries, Leona will make sure Buddy has everything he needs." Including some fun with no coat or booties so he can romp outside like a normal dog. "We have a delicious treat for breakfast. I know you'll both *love* it."

Sarah finally had a bit of color back in her cheeks. She glanced across the café at George who sat staring out the French doors. "I don't know what's gotten into him," she said, more to herself than to Annie or Connie. "Ever since that detective questioned him last night and rummaged through our suitcases, he hasn't said a word to me."

Connie patted Sarah's hand that rested on the table. "Men don't like to talk about their feelings, dear. I think, for them, it's worse than having a tooth pulled without Novocain. Give him his space and he'll come around." She stirred her coffee and sipped a bit off her spoon. "Oh my. This is perfect. Exactly how I like it." She flicked her fingers at Annie. "Go get our breakfast, dear. I'm ravenous."

Annie crouched so she was at the same level with Connie and Sarah. "Before I get your breakfast, I was wondering about what you said when I brought your coffee. You heard one of the investigators say the chef was strangled?"

Connie leaned toward Annie. "That's exactly what I heard. And you know what else?"

Annie waited, knowing Connie couldn't wait to divulge whatever other information she was holding onto.

"They also had a short discussion about Phil, you know, the guy who never made it to the workshop, who died in his car?"

Annie had completely forgotten about him. "What about Phil?"

Connie looked around the café and lowered her voice to a whisper. "They think it might not have been an accident and the two deaths could be connected." She sat back with a satisfied grin.

Annie blinked several times at this new bit of information and made a mental note not to ever share anything with Connie that she didn't want spread around like a spilled drink. "How could that be? Everyone from the workshop was at the Blackbird when Phil died."

"Not everyone." Connie's eyes moved to the counter and the only person sitting there sipping coffee.

Annie turned her head. "Alex?"

"He arrived later out of the blue. Was it merely a coincidence? Didn't you think that was odd?"

Annie had to admit that it *was* an odd coincidence and she certainly had considered the possibility of Alex being the murderer. He had been so helpful with the generator. And he even washed the pots and pans. Was that all just a cover?

Sarah's eyes widened. "And he was upstairs when the chef was murdered."

"Everyone except Leona and myself were upstairs so that's no proof of anything," Annie said. She wondered what the police had found to think there was a connection.

As Annie stood and straightened her legs she felt one of her knees pop. They always complained more in the cold weather. "I'll be back shortly."

She had only gone two steps before she heard her name being called. "Annie? Could we get our breakfast to go?"

Annie saw that Robin hadn't taken her coat or knit beanie off. "Yes, I suppose so. Where are you going?"

Robin smirked. "Back to the Blackbird, of course." She glanced at Jared. "He's going home. The questions last night from the detective were all a bit much for Jared. Well, that and all the guests looking at him sideways every time he even took a breath. They all think you did it, right Jared?" she tapped his head to get him to look up at her.

"You aren't helping any, Robin. I told you to quit being so glib about this. It's serious, and all because of *you* the spotlight is on *me* now. I should never have listened to you—'it will be fun; you can play computer games all weekend; no one will ever know you're even in the room'. Well, that didn't work out like you promised." He slid out of the booth. "Forget the breakfast. I'm not a breakfast person anyway." He shuffled across the café with his head tucked down in his upturned collar, making him look more like a turtle trying to hide than a young man.

"I'll be eating here after all since my ride just slinked out. Can I have his breakfast, too?" Robin asked. "I was up late writing down all this intrigue and it gave me one ginormous appetite."

"No. Jared wasn't actually a guest at the Blackbird so he wasn't entitled to a breakfast to begin with. Aren't you upset even a little that he left?"

Robin shrugged. "Naw. I was getting tired of him anyway. He doesn't have any goals. You know, he's one of those people who always blames someone else when anything goes wrong in his life. Didn't you catch that? He blamed me for being at the Blackbird and getting grilled by the detective. I wasn't the one to tell him to go poking around in all the rooms when we were downstairs. I wasn't even the one to tell him to come—he came up with the idea first."

That made Annie's forehead wrinkle into tight ripples. "Does Detective Crank know he snooped around?"

"She'll figure it out if she hasn't already. Jared's plan was to look for money or prescriptions laying around so he must have left his fingerprints everywhere. He's not careful like I would have been."

Annie slid into the side of the booth that was still warm from Jared. "Did he steal anything?"

Robin shrugged. "I don't know for sure, but it wouldn't surprise me if he did."

"Did he kill Chef Marcel?" The question fell out of Annie's mouth before she could stop herself.

"Don't know the answer to that either. I suppose it's possible that the chef walked in when Jared was in his room and something happened. If I learned anything from what happened last night, it's that Jared is a fool. He would have panicked before he could think of a plan to get his sorry butt out of a jam."

"Why did you sneak him into your room in the first place?" Annie had a hard time squaring Robin's words with her actions. "The way you're talking about him now, it sounds like you don't even like the guy."

Nothing appeared to phase Robin. "Yeah, it seemed like a good idea at the time. Hindsight is always fifty-fifty, isn't it? Take you, for example. You probably wished you'd gone home instead of taking that desperate call from Leona so you wouldn't be involved in this mess."

Annie didn't see that comment coming. "How do you know I wasn't planning to help all along?" This girl was giving Annie the creeps. She knew too much.

Robin tapped her ears. "No one else was paying attention. They were all freaking out about the road conditions when Leona called you. Sure, I only heard one side of the conversation but it wasn't a leap to figure out that she was begging someone to come and then you showed up. Not hard to put that together. So, maybe *everyone* has some regrets now after how the evening went." She tilted her head and raised her eyebrows, challenging Annie to disagree.

She couldn't. The first person who would have the biggest regret would have been Chef Marcel if he was still around to even have that sentiment, Annie thought.

Robin's cool, calm, demeanor unsettled her to the point of forcing her to look away. Robin had been upstairs, too, and could have snuck into the chef's room, and she hadn't wanted to participate in the workshop to begin with. But that certainly wasn't enough of a motive to kill him, was it?

Unlikely.

At any rate, Robin had no trouble spinning theories from the drama at the Blackbird. Did she act on one of her scenarios for her novel?

11

Annie made a tray of the pastry-wrapped, caramel apples to deliver to each of Leona's guests waiting for their breakfasts. She started with Connie and Sarah. Connie was still busy trying to cheer up Sarah to get her mind off of her grumpy husband.

Robin was next. Annie plopped the plate in front of her but she barely noticed with her eyes glued to her phone.

George barely grunted an acknowledgement when Annie offered him the pastry.

"Was that a yes or no?" Annie asked him.

George looked up at Annie as if he'd never seen her before. "What is it?" He wrinkled his nose.

"A pastry-wrapped, caramel-filled baked apple." She forced a smile.

George pushed himself back from the table and stood. He looked down at Annie. "This isn't what was promised for the workshop meals. We were supposed to have our meals at the bed and breakfast, not," he waved his hand around the café, "_this_ place."

Annie used all of her inner resources to ignore his insulting tone. "I'm sure you understand the extenuating circumstances, Mr. Walter. Leona couldn't have foreseen what would happen to Chef Marcel." She was having great difficulty keeping her calm when what she really wanted to do was grab him by the scarf around his neck and wring the snarl off his face. Instead, her smile returned. "I could pack your breakfast and you could take it back to the Blackbird if that works better for you."

"Yeah. Sure. Whatever." He walked to the booth where Connie and Sarah sat.

Annie quickly boxed up the apple pastry, added an egg and cheese croissant, and threw in a blueberry muffin for good measure. It couldn't hurt. By the time she carried it to George he was in the middle of an argument with Sarah.

"Walk for all I care. I'm leaving and you can come or not. You decide." George grabbed the bag from Annie and hustled to the door without looking back.

"Oh dear." Sarah's eyes brimmed to overflowing. "What do I do now?"

"Let him go, dear. No offense or anything, but who wants to spend time with such a grump? I'll give you a ride," Connie offered. "Relax. Enjoy your breakfast. Without the workshop happening, we can stroll up and down Main Street and check out the cute shops. Doesn't that sound nice?"

"What about Buddy?" Sarah asked. "Doesn't he get anxious when you're gone?"

Connie glanced at Annie. "Do you think Leona will mind if I don't get right back like I promised? Sarah could really use some distraction to cheer her up."

"Mind having Buddy around? Not at all. Danny will probably keep him busy outside while he cleans all the paths, brings in firewood, and whatever else needs doing. Don't worry at all." It was a small price to pay on Leona's part for more time without these guests breathing down her neck.

"That's settled then, Sarah. We'll be tourists for the day and it will give George a chance to work through his bad mood."

Annie was glad that Connie had some common sense and expressed exactly what she was thinking. The only difference was that she didn't think George had the ability to work through his bad mood. He had been grumpy from the minute Annie met him the day before.

"He was really looking forward to this workshop, you know," Sarah said, obviously unable to get him out of her mind. "He made the reservations for our Christmas present."

"Oh?" Annie replied. "And you were looking forward to the workshop, too?"

"Well . . ." Sarah stretched out the word. "It wasn't my *first* choice. I was hoping for a cruise, but George said I needed to learn how to make a few fancy desserts."

"*You* needed to learn?" Connie's eyebrows disappeared under her gray bangs. "I hope you told him that he could do the learning himself."

"Oh, I'm not as vocal as you are, Connie." She sighed. "I wish I was sometimes, though."

"If George manages to get a refund, maybe he'll take you on that cruise instead," Annie suggested. She really didn't think there was much hope of getting a refund from a dead guy but she wanted to make Sarah feel a little better.

"The order form said no refunds for any reason so I don't think we'll be seeing that money. And we can't expect poor Leona to give any money back since we *are* staying there and she's providing our meals."

"Right. So, you need to enjoy the weekend anyway. Make the best of the situation. That's what I always tell myself when something gets in the way of my plans. I say, Connie, you never know what this may lead to. It could very well be something *more* fun. So, eat up that pastry so we can enjoy the next part of the breakfast." Connie looked at Annie. "There is more to come, isn't there?"

"Of course. I'll be right back with your breakfast croissant." Annie made a quick detour to the drink cart. She started a fresh pot of coffee and topped off the half and half. The hot beverages always disappeared more quickly during the cold winter weather.

Without turning around, Annie felt warm breath on her neck and a hand on one shoulder. The words whispered in her ear made her shiver. "I love the mocha hot chocolate. Is there any today?"

Annie smiled. "Of course. Would you like to fix you some?"

"Yes, please. You know exactly how I like it," Jason said before he took a step back, allowing Annie to turn and face him. "How's everything going this morning?"

"I suppose it could be worse."

"That bad? There aren't many empty seats this morning. Shouldn't that make it a *good* day?"

Annie handed Jason his mocha hot chocolate with a double dose of whipped cream on top. She lowered her voice. "That's not the problem; it's Leona's guests from the Blackbird who she sent here because they aren't allowed to leave town. Two left without eating, one of which wasn't a real guest anyway. One is in tears. Another is writing her novel which for all I know, includes all the theories of who murdered the chef. At least there's one taking it all in stride. And one more I haven't had a chance to talk to yet." She indicated Alex sitting at the counter. He tapped his fingers on the counter as he sipped his drink as if he was working something through his mind.

Jason grinned. "I see an empty stool next to Alex. Maybe I can coax some conversation out of him. You know, man to man."

Annie whispered in Jason's ear, "Don't tell me you plan to dig for details about the chef's murder?"

"That wasn't my intention at all." The corner of his mouth twitched. "But if the conversation heads in that direction, well, I certainly won't stop him."

Annie squeezed his hand. "Alex came across as a decent guy who helped Leona with the generator and even washed up the pots and pans last night. He said it was because we took him in when he was stranded in the storm, but there's something about him I just can't put my finger on."

"Yoo-hoo, Annie?" Connie's voice rang out in the café. "Did you forget our breakfast croissants?"

Annie rolled her eyes so only Jason could see. "Duty calls."

Jason slowly ambled across the café with his mug and slid onto the stool next to Alex. Annie hurried behind the counter where Greta had the egg and cheese croissant sandwiches waiting. After adding a slice of cantaloupe to each plate, she carried the food to the hungry guests.

"Here you go. Sorry for the wait," she said to Connie and Sarah.

"These look yummy." Connie slid her coffee cup to the edge of the booth. "How about a refill before you get sidetracked again."

"Sure. After I deliver this last croissant to Robin."

Connie swiveled her head around. "She's still here? I thought I saw that stowaway friend of hers slink out. She didn't leave with him?"

"No. Robin is still here." Annie moved to Robin's booth. "Here you go."

She actually tore her eyes away from her phone. "Ah, thanks. I'm going to need a ride back to the bed and breakfast."

"Ask Connie."

"Seriously? She's way too talkative for me. Although, on second thought, it could lead to more interesting fodder for my novel. This weekend has been a goldmine so far."

Annie couldn't help herself. "So, have you decided who the murderer is?"

"Yup, but I'm not revealing anything until I figure out the how."

12

Jason tapped Annie's shoulder and whispered that he'd see her later, just before Connie, Sarah, and Robin left the café. Alex caught her eye and patted the stool next to him, inviting Annie to sit down for a minute.

"Nice place you have here." His comment contained admiration.

"This café belongs to Leona but she twisted my arm to run it for her when she needed more time for the Blackbird Bed and Breakfast. Well, along with my mom and Greta." Annie nodded toward each woman giving them their due recognition. "And, some days, they pull more of the weight around here than I do with all the distractions."

"Regardless, it's a jewel. My bad luck yesterday turned into good fortune today. As you can see," he pointed to the pastry in front of him, "I begged shamelessly for a second pastry and Greta took pity on me." He lowered his nose to the pastry and inhaled deeply. "The sweet surprise inside has turned my mouth into a watery pit, drooling for more."

Annie couldn't help but chuckle at Alex's description. She

leaned closer. "You've been keeping that stool warm for a long time. Is the ambiance that mesmerizing?"

"I've been patiently waiting for a word with you. I thought Connie and her entourage would never leave."

That comment startled Annie. "Why me? Did you hear something interesting last night after I left?"

He slid a big chunk of the pastry into his mouth. An eyebrow twitch and a slight nod told Annie he had something to tell her but she had to be patient while he enjoyed this treat.

After a satisfied sigh he set his fork on the plate. "I'm starting to think that you and that friendly husband of yours make quite the tag team."

"What—"

"Don't worry. My comment is completely complimentary. Jason wasn't quite as blunt as you are, but I had the distinct impression that he was trying to figure out who the heck I am and what I might know." Alex managed another bite while he let Annie figure out her response.

It didn't take her long. "So, what *is* your story?" This conversation had taken a decidedly strange turn.

He savored his pastry. "I'd rather not get into it here." He turned to look at Annie. "Could we get together when you're done working?"

"Answer me this—was it an accident that you ended up at the Blackbird Bed and Breakfast last night?" Annie stared at Alex. She didn't know why the answer to that question was important, but if it was his planned destination all along she wanted to know why. And it would ratchet him up higher on the suspect list.

He met her gaze and gave a slight shake of his head. "Not exactly. Where shall we meet?"

Before Annie gave him directions to Cobblestone Cottage, she sent Jason a text to see if he thought it was a good idea to invite Alex to their house. He replied quickly, saying yes, invite him for dinner.

Annie looked up from her phone.

"Did Jason agree?" The edges of his eyes crinkled with amusement. "I told you that you two make a good team."

His comment completely unnerved Annie. "He did." She gave Alex directions to their house. "Come around five so we can talk before dinner."

"Dinner is even part of the plan? How lucky am I?"

"Well, if Jason is cooking you might not want to bring too big of an appetite. He's a vegetarian but he *does* make a killer salad. He has also been known to fill the house with smoke while trying to cook much of anything in the oven."

"Unfortunately, as a man I can relate to that, at least the burning food part. How about this? I'll stop somewhere and bring dinner. It's the least I can do after your kind invitation. Is there a pizza place in town?"

"You can get pizza to go from Fitzwilly's Tavern. That will go well with Jason's salad." Annie slid off the stool. "I'll bring dessert."

With that, Alex's eyes brightened. "More of these apple pastries?"

"No. I think they're gone, but don't worry, all of the desserts from the Black Cat Café are mouthwateringly delicious."

Alex used his fork to scrape up the last bits of caramel off the plate before he wiped his mouth and slid off the stool. He straightened slowly, a condition from sitting for so long Annie decided.

"If you're heading back to the Blackbird now, be sure to tell Leona that the apple pastries were a huge hit. She'll need to hear something positive to get through another long day and night with the guests and no workshop activity to distract them."

"Leona doesn't have to entertain anyone. She's running a bed and breakfast, not a babysitting motel."

"But she only opened on the first of the year and this pastry workshop was her first event. She had high hopes for positive feedback to bring in more business. And now, with a murder right in one of the rooms," Annie shook her head, "it's going to be hard to bounce back from *that* headline."

"Certainly not her fault. People have short memories." Alex shrugged into his thick parka. "Pizza for three?"

Annie laughed. "You never know who might show up so bring extra."

After Alex left the café, there were only a few stragglers remaining. The rush was over.

"Who was that?" Mia asked when Annie carried a stack of dirty dishes to the sink.

"Alex—he was at the Blackbird last night."

"One of the workshop attendees?"

"Not exactly. He said his car got stranded and he hiked to the Blackbird. During the storm. That part is true, but he indicated that it wasn't an accident to end up on the Blackbird's doorstep. He's bringing pizza over for dinner tonight and he said he'll share his story." She stacked the dishes in the dishwasher and turned it on.

"What kind of story?"

Annie shrugged. "I have no idea but I suspect it *could* have something to do with Chef Marcel and the workshop. Why else would he be heading to the Blackbird during a storm without a reservation? Something is strange about Alex's reason for being in town."

"You're making a lot of assumptions about this guy. If you're right, he could be dangerous. Did you think of that?" Mia asked.

"Jason sat with him here earlier and they talked. It was his suggestion to invite Alex over for dinner. It's not like I'm meeting him in a dark, isolated spot. Why don't you join us, too, if that will keep you from worrying."

Mia grinned. "I was afraid you'd never ask. I'll bring something for dessert."

"Perfect, that gets me off the hook. Now all I need to do is pack up some cookies for Thelma." Annie untied her apron. "You and Greta are all set? Tomorrow is Sunday. I'm looking forward to the later brunch opening time."

Mia looked at Greta. "Anything else before Annie leaves?"

"Nope. I'm planning to make more of the pastry-wrapped apples. They were a huge hit. The breakfast croissants along with our normal assortment of muffins, scones, and sweet breads should satisfy anyone who stops by." Greta put two pans of muffins on a cooling rack. "Oh, I almost forgot. When Detective Crank and Police Chief Johnson were waiting at the cash register, I heard them talking about the guy who was found dead in his car. They were whispering, but I'm positive I heard them mention that they are looking into it being a poisoning."

"Well, that's more details than what Connie told me. She overheard the police talking last night that both the deaths could be linked. Phil was on his way to the workshop at the Blackbird so there is that connection, but what else could there be?" Annie twisted her scarf around her neck. "I hope Alex has some answers tonight."

"You should ask Camilla to come, too," Mia suggested. "Men seem to throw caution to the wind when she's around and turns on her charm."

"Her flirting, you mean?" Annie laughed. "That's a great idea. I'll stop by her jewelry shop before I drive home. Maybe Leona can slip away, too. I'm sure she'd like to come if Danny is okay taking over for an hour or two."

"I'll swing by the Blackbird and give her a head's up. What's on the menu, anyway?" Mia placed an apple crumb cake in a box.

"Alex is bringing pizza. I told him not to be surprised if there were a few extra people besides me and Jason. Is that what you're bringing for dessert?"

Mia nodded.

"Perfect. I have vanilla ice cream to go with it. I love it when a plan falls into place. See you later." Annie zipped her coat and headed into the February cold.

A brisk walk from the Black Cat Café to the Velvet Box to see Camilla stretched Annie's legs and cleared out the stale air in her lungs. Each breath out created a frosty puff around her face. Cars swooshed by spraying slush to the side of the road which kept her close to the buildings so as not to get splattered.

Annie pulled the door of the Velvet Box open. The bell tinkled a friendly greeting. Camilla, Annie's friend, looked up. As Camilla looked beyond the shoulder of her customer, the light bounced off her eyes matching the green streak through her blonde hair.

A slight pink crept into Camilla's cheeks. That was odd, thought Annie, until the customer turned around. Tyler's face also held a healthy glow of pink and his earlier comment about a new friend fell into place. More like a crash, actually.

"Time for me to get back to work," Tyler said to break the awkward silence. The bell tinkled and the door silently closed behind him.

"You and Tyler?" Annie heard the shock in her own voice and immediately regretted how it must sound.

A flash of something—annoyance or possibly anger—passed over Camilla's face. "It's about time you found out. Tyler has been slinking around like a naughty boy." Camilla's hands moved around with her words. "I told him he was being ridiculous. At least now maybe he'll accept that you've moved on and he can, too."

"Of course. I mean, he's a great guy." It was Annie's turn to feel heat travel into her cheeks. "I suppose it surprised me because there was no need to hide your relationship with Tyler."

"That's exactly what I told him." Camilla ran her fingers through her hair and walked around the counter to stand next to Annie. "It's not a problem for you, is it?"

Annie hugged her friend. "I hope you know me better than

that. I'm happy for you. For both of you. It's time Tyler moves on, and," she laughed, "you'll probably be the best thing to happen to him."

"You mean it?" Camilla's eyes opened into wide spheres.

"Oh yes. You are the *perfect* person to bring fun and laughter into his life, which is a stark contrast from working on all the police cases in Catfish Cove. By the way, I love your new hair color."

"Tyler loves it, too." She swung her head, making the ends of her blonde hair graze her shoulders. "I thought he might be shocked by the green streak but he said he loves how it matches my eyes. Well, my colored contacts."

"So, what were you two lovebirds talking about when I came in?" Annie wiggled her eyebrows.

"Um, I guess this will be the awkward part for me."

"Why is that? Did Tyler ask you to spy on me or something?" Annie laughed.

Camilla frowned.

"You're kidding. Listen, Camilla. I value your friendship, but somehow you need to figure out where to draw the boundaries." Annie's jaw clenched.

"It works both ways, Annie. You can't expect me to tell you something Tyler shares with me in confidence."

Annie waved her hand dismissively. "That's a given. So, listen, I stopped by to see if you want to come over for pizza tonight at my place."

Camilla's eyes lit up. "Really? I'd love to. Tyler said that with these murders he'd be busy until he doesn't know when."

"*Murders*? With an *s*?"

"Oh dear. This is going to be so much harder than I imagined. You always find out stuff anyway, but please don't tell him you heard that from me. Okay?"

Annie's hand rested on Camilla's arm. "Don't worry." This

rumor was already in circulation so it wasn't exactly a secret, but now she had confirmation right from the police chief's mouth.

She left the Velvet Box wondering what else, if anything, Camilla knew about the two murders. This blossoming relationship between Tyler and Camilla presented something new for Annie to think about on many levels as she made her way back down Main Street.

Annie couldn't keep herself from wondering if Camilla and Tyler made a good match. On the one hand, Camilla's energy and enthusiasm for life couldn't be anything but a positive in a relationship. But, on the other hand, if Camilla got bored with Tyler's, not so much dull, but reserved personality, it would break his heart if she left him.

Oh dear. Annie was surprised that she still carried this responsibility for Tyler's feelings but she'd known him for too long to not care. And, since *she* broke his heart when she ran off during their engagement, she didn't want Tyler to suffer a second time.

Would this development add an awkward, at best, layer in her relationship with Camilla? Annie shook her head and decided she would treat Camilla exactly the same as always and if Camilla felt uncomfortable, it would be up to *her* to adjust.

Annie smiled and a bit of the heaviness weighing her down lifted. One problem solved in the short time it took to walk to her car. If only every problem was that easy to solve, she wouldn't have butterflies in her stomach wondering what information Alex was going to share tonight.

13

Roxy danced around Annie's legs as soon as she got home. The fireplace logs crackled with an irresistible invitation to snuggle on the couch with her and the two cats.

Smokey lifted his head and flicked the end of his tail but Snowball only tucked her nose deeper into the warmth of her own fur. Oh, to be a cat on a cold wintry afternoon with a toasty spot for a nap, Annie thought.

Unfortunately, Roxy had other plans and it didn't include letting Annie relax with the cats in front of the fire. She whined and looked toward the porch door.

"I did take her out not too long ago," Jason said as he walked out of his office.

Annie held up a box of cookies. "I do need to visit Thelma and deliver this."

Roxy barked when Annie mentioned her elderly neighbor's name.

"That's what's on your agenda, too?" Annie asked Roxy. "Probably because you know she always has a yummy dog treat for you."

"Don't be long. When is our dinner guest arriving?"

"I told him five and he's bringing pizza so all you need to make is a salad." Annie didn't miss the relieved expression on Jason's face. She laughed. "I guess that plan sounds good?"

"Uh-huh. Salads are my specialty. No chance of burning anything," he joked.

"And I might have invited some others, too."

Roxy scratched at the door impatiently.

"Let me guess—Mia, Camilla, and Leona?"

"Well, Mia and Camilla for sure. I'm not sure if Leona can get away." Annie reached for the doorknob. "Oh, and did you know that Tyler and Camilla are an item?"

Jason's mouth dropped open. "Really? I don't know why I'm surprised except that we didn't hear anything before now. Camilla isn't the best at keeping secrets. She'd be great for Tyler."

"I think so too, but I'm afraid my relationship with Camilla could become awkward at times. She already let it slip that Tyler's working on two murders and will be busy."

"Two?"

"Chef Marcel and the workshop no-show, Phil, who was found dead in his car. It wasn't the first I heard of it but this confirms the rumor." She pulled the door open and Roxy darted out and streaked to the Lake Trail. "I won't be long," she hollered over her shoulder as she left to catch up with Roxy.

Roxy made a beeline along the Lake Trail straight to the path that led to Thelma's house. Annie could just make out Thelma's profile in the fading light. She waved.

Annie opened the kitchen door and Roxy zoomed through as soon as the opening cracked far enough for her trim body to squeeze inside. Annie followed. She left her snowy boots on the mat and hung her coat on a hook. "Hello, Thelma."

"I'm so happy you stopped by, Annie. You and my favorite four-legged friend. Here you go, Roxy," Thelma's voice rang out from the next room.

Even before Annie entered the living room she could imagine

the scene. She chuckled to herself. She knew exactly what Thelma and Roxy were up to. As she entered Thelma's warm living room, the familiar scene that met her eyes was exactly as she expected. Thelma sat in her comfy chair with a view of Heron Lake. An afghan and her big Maine coon cat, Moby, were draped over her legs. Roxy lay on the rug in front of Thelma, enjoying a dog treat.

"I brought you a surprise." Annie set the box on the table next to Thelma's chair.

"You brought me three surprises—you, Roxy, and whatever deliciousness is in that box." Thelma smiled.

"Shall I make you some tea?"

"That would be wonderful. And tell me the latest news, too."

Annie turned on the tea kettle. The latest news was murder, but did Thelma want to hear about that?

"My son already told me what happened at Leona's Blackbird Bed and Breakfast. Do you have more details?" Well, that answered Annie's question.

"Not really." She poured hot water over Thelma's herbal teabag and returned to the living room. "Here you go." She set the cup next to the Black Cat Café box.

"I can't wait another second to see what's in here." Thelma carefully moved the box onto her lap next to Moby and lifted the lid. "Oh, my. You do always manage to spoil me rotten." Thelma looked at Annie with a big smile on her face. "And, I'm not complaining about it, either, my dear friend." She chose a horn shaped cookie covered in almonds and with one end dipped in chocolate. "Would you like one, too?"

Annie held her hands up. "No thanks. Those almond cookies are all for you. Company is coming for dinner so I'd better save my appetite."

Thelma's hand stopped halfway to her mouth. "You might want to change your mind about spoiling your appetite if Jason is cooking."

Annie laughed. "No. I don't have to worry about a house full of smoke. Jason is making a salad and our guest is bringing pizza."

"Oh, good." The cookie made it to Thelma's mouth. She nibbled, closed her eyes, and leaned her head against the back of her chair.

Annie waited for Thelma to savor the treat. There was no rushing her friend when it came to anything sweet.

"So, who's your guest? Anyone I know?" Thelma asked after the cookie had disappeared.

"No. His name is Alex Harmon and he showed up on the Blackbird's doorstep during the storm last night. Leona unexpectedly had a room available."

"Was that the room meant for the poor man who died in his car on the way to the workshop? My son told me all about what happened. As a matter of fact, after photos of both of those men who died were on the news, my son realized he had seen them."

That comment piqued Annie's attention.

"My son was waiting in a booth at the Bigger Burger fast food place he frequents more often than he should, in my opinion. Anyway, he was there yesterday afternoon." Thelma sipped her tea before she helped herself to another cookie.

Annie let Thelma's words run through her brain a second time before she grasped the meaning. "Your son saw both men? They randomly happened to be in the restaurant at the same time?"

"Oh no, they came in together, sat together, and my son even heard them arguing." She used her pinky to wipe a crumb from the edge of her mouth. "He said that he had to wait quite a while for his order to be ready. So much for *fast food*."

"He's sure about who he saw?" This information didn't make sense unless Chef Marcel and Phil already knew each other. That was possible, she decided.

"Yes. Positive. He even caught their names—Phil and Marcel.

It's mostly the same clientele that goes to Bigger Burger so they stuck out like obvious out-of-towners. The argument ended when Phil told Marcel to pay up or the whole deal was over." Thelma scrunched her eyes and looked at Annie. "What do you suppose that could mean?"

"I don't know." But she intended to find out. "Did your son hear anything else?"

"You know, he said at the time he only listened with one ear but after he saw on the news that they were dead, he tried to remember exactly everything he heard. The only other bit was that as the guy named Marcel got up to leave, he bought the other guy some sort of beverage and told him to wait for it to cool down and not to follow right away."

"Did your son tell all this to the police?"

"I don't know. Do you think he should?"

"Yes. The police always say that any bit of information could be useful even if it doesn't seem important." Annie stood. "I'd better get home before Jason sends a posse out after me."

Thelma laughed. "He would, wouldn't he? Except you have Roxy with you so he might not worry quite as much as if you were out all alone." Thelma picked up her newspaper. "Do you have half a minute to help me with my crossword puzzle before you head out into the cold?"

"Sure. What's the theme today?"

"It's right up your alley—cookies." Thelma helped herself to a third cookie. "This is the one that has me stumped. The clue is, kids' favorite." She looked at Annie. "I thought it should be chocolate chip, but that doesn't fit. The fourth letter is an n and there's a space after the sixth letter." She let the paper fall on top of Moby who couldn't care less. "Any ideas?"

"Well, I would agree with you but since chocolate chip doesn't fit, the next most asked for cookie at the café for kids would be peanut butter. Does that fit?"

Thelma, using her pen, filled in the squares. "It does! You

always figure out the tough ones. Thank you." Thelma rested her head against the back of her chair. "And thanks for the cookies," she mumbled.

Annie tiptoed out with Roxy close behind. She left Thelma with her eyes closed and a smile on her face. They headed into the cold for a brisk walk back home. She pushed the porch door open and followed Roxy into her toasty living room.

The warmth from the fire was a welcome contrast against her chilled cheeks.

"Here's Annie," Annie heard Jason say as she closed the door behind her. "It's time to come clean about why you're in town."

Jason's words made her stop in her tracks, a sense of foreboding sending a shiver down her spine.

14

"**W**ho *are* you?" Annie asked, not meaning Alex's name, but wanting to know his background. She stood rooted to the mat just inside the door, her parka zipped to her chin. Sweat trickled down inside her layers but she ignored her rising body temperature.

Alex looked like a man who controlled his world. The gray sprinkled through his thick, dark, and a-bit-too-long hair gave him a casual-on-purpose look. His face, with a few noticeable lines, gave Annie the impression he had seen his share of problems. All in all, his image tonight contrasted one hundred percent from the almost frozen man she saw standing on the Blackbird's front door the previous night.

"Get out of your parka before you roast," Jason said.

She unzipped her parka and slid her feet out of her boots. The smell of pizza hit her nose. Her stomach rumbled. Was food Alex's bribe to warm them up to trust him? Was there even a reason she should be suspicious of this man who appeared just before a murder happened?

There wasn't an obvious reason but she *was* suspicious, she realized, as she moved further into the warm room.

"How's Thelma?" Jason asked.

"Well, after devouring a handful of cookies that I brought, she needed to take a little nap."

Jason chuckled. "She does have a sweet tooth, doesn't she?"

"And, her son relayed an interesting conversation he heard between Phil and Chef Marcel," Annie casually added.

Alex's forehead wrinkled. "Did her son know them?"

"No. Did *you*?" Annie's voice came out more accusatory than she intended but, at this point, she didn't want to beat around the bush with her guest. "What *is* going on with you?" She looked from Jason to Alex. If he was somehow connected to Chef Marcel, she wanted to know. If he wasn't, well, then she'd be able to relax and enjoy his food offering.

"It's not what you think," Alex began.

Not a denial, she noticed. "So, you're a mind reader now?" Annie clenched her jaw. Between Robin and now Alex, she had about enough of people assuming they knew what she was thinking. Alex and his condescending comment pushed her normally-calm demeanor over the edge. Who did he think he was? Did he suspect that Annie eyed him with suspicion as the possible murderer?

Jason sighed. "Give him a chance to explain before you jump to any conclusions, Annie."

She plopped down on the couch. Roxy jumped next to her. "I'm all ears." She would listen, but at this point she couldn't imagine anything he could say that would justify his sudden appearance the night before. No matter how she cut it, Alex was a suspect.

Alex cleared his throat. He licked his lips. "You'll hear this eventually, anyway." He paused. "My plan was to stay well under the radar; come into town, do my thing, and leave."

"And what *thing* were you planning to do? Kill someone and leave before the body was discovered?"

"I can see how you might have jumped to that conclusion but, no, murder was never part of my plan."

"Plans can take unexpected turns."

"True, and the storm did throw a curveball. That's why I wanted to talk to you about why I came to town. I need some help and I have to come up with a new plan."

Annie crossed her legs and her arms as if this would let him know his words weren't having any impact on her.

"You see, Annie, I'm a private investigator."

Okay. She didn't see *that* coming. She looked at Jason and knew shock was written all over her face.

Jason chuckled. "I checked his background and he's telling the truth."

Before Alex had time to explain what he was in town investigating, the door opened blowing cold air, Mia, and Camilla inside.

Mia set her Black Cat Café box with dessert on the counter after she shed her warm clothes. Camilla added a bottle of cabernet next to the dessert on her way to warm herself in front of the fire.

"Alex, this is my friend, Camilla, and you already saw my mom, Mia, at the café," Annie said. "Mom, Camilla, meet Alex. He got stranded in the storm and ended up at the Blackbird last night."

"One of the suspects?" Camilla blurted out. She covered her mouth with her fingers. "Sorry, that just slipped out. I need to watch what I say or I'll be in heaps of trouble with Tyler." She looked at Annie. "What? You know now so why do you have that shocked look on your face?"

Annie waved Camilla's words away. "It's not what you said. It's something else."

"Okay. I'm opening this wine. Who else wants a glass? Does it even go with pizza?" Camilla blabbered nervously.

"Sure," Alex said. "Here," he took the bottle from Camilla, "let me."

Jason handed Alex the opener and Annie put glasses on the counter.

"So, you came for the pastry workshop?" Camilla asked after Alex handed her a full glass of wine. "Leona sure was excited about hosting Chef Marcel, but *that* turned into a disaster for her."

"No. I happened to get stuck in a snow drift not far from the Blackbird. Annie and Leona kindly found a room for me." Alex handed wine around the room.

"I thought it was a private event and fully booked." Camilla slapped the side of her head with the palm of her hand. "Right. One of the participants never made it."

"You seem to know a lot, Camilla," Alex said.

"Not really. It's just that my boyfriend has been working on this and I've heard some information. Not any important details, just some mumbling and grumbling when he was on the phone with Detective Crank."

Alex caught Annie's eye and lifted an eyebrow.

"Right. I should have explained," Annie said. "Camilla is dating the chief of police."

"You're the guy Tyler said is here to complicate his life?" Camilla gnawed on her fingernail. She took a long gulp of wine. "I just keep sticking my foot in my mouth, don't I?" She finished her wine, set her glass on the counter, and looked at Annie. "I didn't think it would be so complicated to date Tyler and still hang out with you. I'm going home before something else falls out of my mouth that I'll regret."

"No need for that," Alex said, heading for the door and his coat. "You are all friends. If anyone leaves, it should be me."

"That won't solve my problem. You aren't the only one who I need to be careful around." Camilla bundled up. "No offense,

Annie, but this just isn't working for me tonight." She opened the door and disappeared into the darkness.

"That was awkward," Annie said. "Camilla is in a tough spot since all of us here know Tyler too well. This relationship has put her between a rock and a hard place."

"Why is the police chief telling his girlfriend stuff that's confidential?" Alex asked. "If you ask me, he's the one who should be careful with what he shares."

"So far Camilla hasn't shared anything I haven't heard elsewhere, but she doesn't know that. I'm sure Tyler is completely professional around her."

Jason carried plates to the table along with the two pizzas Alex had brought. A big mixed greens salad with loads of other veggies was the centerpiece on the table. "Is anyone else hungry for some pizza?"

"I thought we'd never get to enjoy what Alex brought," Annie said. "And I see that he got one of my favorites—pesto with broccoli, onions, and mushrooms. Maybe you do read minds, after all." She hated to admit it to herself, but the food had managed to soften her opinion of Alex. Slightly. It wouldn't kill her to at least listen to what he had to say . . . while she enjoyed the pizza.

The edges of Alex's eyes wrinkled. "Yes, that's one of my super powers, especially when I got a bit of help from the waitress, Hailey, who said she knows you well. Once I mentioned where I was going, she told me what to bring with no ifs, ands, or buts about it."

Annie laughed. "And what else did she tell you about me?" Maybe it was the wine helping her to relax.

Alex pulled his thumb and finger across his lips. "I swore on penalty of death *not* to reveal those secrets."

After everyone made themselves comfortable and loaded their plates with food, Annie decided that she'd waited long enough to ask Alex the question that was eating at her. "So, why *are* you in town?"

He finished chewing and swallowing before he leaned back in his chair. "Like I told you already, I'm a private investigator." He focused on the pizza in front of him as if it was the most fascinating serving of food he'd ever had the chance to enjoy.

"Yes. A private investigator that just *happened* to show up at the Blackbird Bed and Breakfast where a well-known chef was murdered? That smells like an awfully big coincidence. Especially when you've already admitted that it was sort of your intention to be there." Annie leaned back in her chair and kept her eyes fixed on Alex.

"The Blackbird Bed and Breakfast was not my original destination."

"Let's quit dancing around your intention. The fact that you arrived in Catfish Cove to investigate something and you did end up at the Blackbird puts you right at the scene of a murder. You're a suspect whether you like it or not."

"I suppose you're a suspect too, Annie," Alex countered.

"And it's not the first time, unfortunately, but we're talking about you, not me. You wanted to have this conversation. So let's have it."

Alex's eyebrows danced up his forehead but he didn't say anything.

Annie stared.

Alex sighed. "I have to admit, you're tougher than being questioned by Detective Crank . . . and she was tough."

"I've been under Detective Crank's glare many times so I certainly take that as a big compliment."

The conversation and eating around the table came to a standstill as Annie and Alex played their game of cat and mouse.

"You have managed to talk about everything but what I thought you came here to talk about." Annie leaned forward and looked at Alex who sat across the table from her. "Let me be blunt. Who did you come to town to investigate?"

After more wine, Alex said, "It wasn't a *who*, it was a group of people."

"Who are you working *for*?"

Alex looked around the table. "I'm hoping you'll help me."

Annie waited. Not one muscle twitched as she stared at Alex.

"Chef Marcel." Alex's words sucked the air from the room like a noose squeezed tight. "Chef Marcel hired me."

15

"Chef Marcel? You were working for Chef Marcel?" Annie blurted out. "Why?"

"All I can tell you is that he called me about a week ago and asked me to meet him here in Catfish Cove. He said he had a problem with someone and he'd give me the rest of the details when I arrived."

"But he was murdered before you got any of those details," Annie stated as that reality fell into place. She slumped against the back of her chair.

"I'm not sure who else noticed the chef's shock when you introduced me to everyone after you let me in last night. I think he covered it pretty quickly and no one made a connection between the two of us. To be honest, I only wanted to see where the Blackbird was, then I planned to stay somewhere else and contact him. But," he raised both hands, palms up in a gesture of complete hopelessness, "when my car got stuck in the middle of the storm, my only choice was to walk to the Blackbird. Believe me, it wasn't where I'd planned to spend the night."

"And you never got a chance to talk to him and get more information?"

Alex shook his head. "I already told you about how I heard his door open and close several times. I assumed someone was in his room. I was hoping to find a chance to catch him away from everyone at some point, but you know how *that* turned out. And once Leona locked his door, I didn't want to risk going in to have a look around."

Annie ran her fingers through her strawberry blonde curls. This turn of events had the potential to change her whole outlook on Alex. If it was all the truth. At least on the surface, Alex had no reason to kill the chef. "Wow. Did you tell all this to Detective Crank?"

Alex nodded. "I had to. She had me pegged as one of the suspects, maybe even the top one. I suppose I still am on her list, but maybe not as high after I told her that I was working for the chef and he was already worried for his life."

"Believe me, everyone at the Blackbird is on her list. Detective Crank doesn't rule anyone out until they have an airtight alibi with zero possibility of even the slightest chance of a motive. And, she could think you're lying." Annie added that as an afterthought, since it was a possibility.

"So, I'm a suspect until the case is solved?"

"Pretty much," Annie said.

Questions flew at Alex from every direction as Annie let herself think about this new turn of events.

"You came to investigate all the participants?" she asked. "Do you have any idea how Phil fit into Chef Marcel's agenda? From what my neighbor told me, it sounded like when her son saw them at Bigger Burger, he had the impression that they weren't strangers to each other."

Alex drummed his fingers on the table. "Marcel hinted that he had a partner but it wasn't going smoothly. Maybe that was Phil?"

"But Phil was one of the participants," Annie said. "Or was it designed to only *look* that way?"

"And someone killed both of them," Jason added. "A disgruntled customer who happened to know they were working together?"

"A someone or someones?" Annie emphasized the possibility of more than one person. "Whoever murdered the chef *had* to be someone staying at the Blackbird and if they were at the Blackbird they couldn't have killed Phil, too. Unless," Annie looked at Alex, "that person hadn't arrived at the Blackbird until later."

"And since *I* didn't kill Phil," Alex said, "I have to assume that there are two murderers."

Annie shivered. "Unless we have Phil's time of death wrong?" She shook her head. "That's something for the police to figure out. We can come up with all kinds of theories, but it's just a big guessing game on our part."

Mia stacked the empty dinner plates and carried them to the kitchen. She returned with her dessert. "Maybe something sweet will help the old brain cells see everything differently. You said you have ice cream, Annie?"

"I do." She made no move to get it.

Jason jumped up from the table. "I'll get it, along with plates and forks. What did you bring, Mia?"

"Apple crumb cake, a perfect comfort dessert for cold weather." She scooped out big portions onto four plates while Jason added a dollop of vanilla ice cream.

Just as Annie slid a spoonful of ice cream and apple crumb cake into her mouth, the door opened, letting a gust of cold air in along with her aunt.

"Thanks for waiting for me," Leona said, not even trying to hide her sarcastic tone. She dumped her coat and boots at the door. "Did you save some dessert for me at least?"

"Make yourself comfortable." Jason got a fifth plate for Leona. He let her add her own amount of dessert while he poured her a glass of wine. It wasn't a stretch to assume she'd want the wine after all the drama at the Blackbird.

"I wasn't sure you'd manage to get away," Annie said. "How are your guests doing tonight?"

Leona rolled her eyes. "I had Buddy all day while Connie played tourist. He's sweet but wants to be cuddled constantly and I had cleaning and cooking to do. I suppose it was a small price to pay to have her out of my hair, though. She's one high maintenance woman. Sarah isn't any bother. She just frets and wrings her hands and George stayed in their room. I was thankful I didn't have to look at his grumpy face all afternoon. Robin comes and goes like a ghost and I suppose you know that her loser boyfriend flew the coop." She glared at Alex. "The only *helpful* guest bailed on me." She had a healthy sip of wine.

"That's not fair. I filled the woodbin before I came over here," Alex said. "You insisted that you had everything under control before I left."

"Yeah, yeah, yeah. You had those sad puppy dog eyes and I felt sorry for you. I knew I couldn't leave and I didn't have the heart to ask you to stick around to help with *my* problems when it was obvious that you had somewhere so much more inviting to escape to."

Annie laughed at Leona and Alex's banter. The more she was around the guy, the more her attitude toward him softened. "Did you leave Danny in charge tonight?"

"Uh-huh." Leona wiped her mouth with the back of her hand. "As soon as dinner was served, he told me to take a break and he'd do the clean-up. I think he could tell I was at the end of my rope. Plus, he won't be around tomorrow to help."

Annie hid her laugh behind a fake cough. Of course Danny could read Leona's mood like a cheap novel.

"So, here I am." She dove into the apple crumb cake like she hadn't eaten all day. "This is pretty good," Leona said between bites. "Did you make it, Annie?"

"No. You did and you know it."

Leona grinned. "After hearing that my quiche wasn't warm

enough and the pot roast was too dry, I have to get my compliments where I can. Even if I have to give them to myself." She patted her stomach and finally let a smile spread across her face. "I'm so glad to be away from those people for a while. Fill me in on what you've heard about the chef?"

"Just a few rumors floating around town. Oh," Annie said, "and guess who Camilla is making flirty eyes at now?"

Leona looked around the table. "I was wondering why she wasn't here. Who's the lucky guy?"

"Police Chief Johnson."

Leona choked and sputtered on the wine she had just attempted to swallow. "Tyler? That's *great*. She'll be able to fill us in on anything she hears about the investigation. Right?"

Everyone sitting at the table laughed at Leona's assumption.

"Not on purpose," Annie said. "She couldn't get out of here fast enough after she accidentally said a couple of things she wished she had kept to herself. Unfortunately, what she said wasn't anything I hadn't already heard elsewhere."

"Camilla is going to keep a low profile with us so she doesn't create waves with Tyler? Good luck with that," Leona said. "He can't expect her to give up all her friends. That's not a relationship worth anything. By the way, he came to the Blackbird today looking for the stow-away."

"Jared? What for?" Alex asked.

Leona crunched her eyebrows at Alex. "You seem awfully interested for a random bystander."

"He's not exactly a random bystander, Leona."

Puckered lips joined the crunched eyebrows on Leona's face as she stared at Alex.

"We haven't had time to get into all the details yet, but Alex is a private investigator working, or, more accurately, he *was* working for Chef Marcel," Annie explained. "I guess that detail got overlooked when you arrived."

Leona's jaw dropped and her eyebrows shot up. Then she

grinned. "Well, doesn't that just take the cake . . . and maybe the ice cream, too. I'll bet hearing about Alex's career made Detective Crank's already bad day a bit worse. She wouldn't like the idea of anyone overlapping into *her* territory." She rubbed her hands together. "What a shame." The sarcasm and glee in her voice was unmistakable. "So, are you ready to hear my plan for tomorrow?"

"Of course." Annie pushed the apple crumb cake closer to Leona. "Have some more."

Leona didn't hesitate. "I don't eat much when there are guests staying at the Blackbird—my stomach gets tied in knots." She added ice cream to the crumb cake on her plate—two scoops. "Okay. I know I'll go crazy with everyone just hanging around the Blackbird until Detective Crank says they can leave; and, they've paid through Monday morning; plus, the chef has all his ingredients in my kitchen for his pastry lessons."

"You're going to do some teaching?" Annie asked. She knew her aunt too well.

"Uh-huh," she mumbled around her mouthful of dessert, then swallowed. "Why not? What's to lose at this point? It will be good practice for me. If all goes well, I can run workshops myself instead of depending on some annoying chef that just gets himself killed anyway." She looked around the table. "I'll need some help, of course." That comment was directed at Annie.

Annie forced her face to remain neutral.

"Could I take Phil's spot?" Alex asked. "I'll call it my new plan —a way to watch and listen to all the guests and hopefully gather some clues."

Leona grinned. "That would be perfect." She pushed herself back from the table and patted her stomach. "Delicious, if I don't say so myself. See you tomorrow, Annie. Mia and Greta can handle the Black Cat Café by themselves."

Leona bundled herself up. "I told Danny I wouldn't be gone for long. He's not crazy about being in charge of the guests all by himself." She opened the door and left as quickly as she had arrived.

"Don't worry about anything, Annie," Mia said. "Leona is right, Greta and I will be fine on our own tomorrow."

Alex stood. "I can't wait to hang out with all the suspects while I attempt to learn some baking techniques. This is turning out to be one of my more interesting jobs."

"Except you might not get paid," Annie added.

"Actually, Chef Marcel deposited a nice retainer in my bank account. I guess I owe him to find his killer."

"My advice?" Annie said to Alex. "Stay out of Detective Crank's way. She doesn't take kindly to anyone treading in her territory."

Alex nodded. "No problem with that while I'm rolling out pastry dough and drizzling chocolate with the suspects. I couldn't ask for a better cover."

With that comment, Alex slipped into his warm clothes, saluted to the others, and let himself out.

"He's right, you know," Jason said to Annie. "What better way to watch all the suspects and listen for motives? Leona just handed you a gift and you didn't even realize it."

Annie let herself relax. With Alex working undercover, she'd be another set of eyes and ears listening to what everyone had to say. "I guess so. Leona came up with a great plan . . . even if she sees it as a way to keep her sanity."

They laughed.

16

At least when Annie rolled out of bed Sunday morning, the temperature was heading into the low forties with no breeze and a clear sky on the horizon. With sunshine and rising mercury, Annie decided it was a February heat wave.

"I think I'll bring Roxy to the Blackbird. She can keep Buddy occupied so he doesn't get underfoot during Leona's baking class," Annie told Jason as they sat at the kitchen counter with their morning coffees. "The less distractions for Leona, the better."

"I suppose Danny will be outside or in his workshop with his new project so he can keep an eye on the dogs."

"Actually, he's only around for the morning. What new project?" She wrapped her hands around her warm coffee cup.

"He's making a cherry framed mirror for Leona. Don't spoil the secret."

"Not me." Annie drained her coffee cup. "I'm not sure if I'll be home for dinner tonight. I might just stay and help Leona with the meal at the Blackbird. You could come too if you want. Maybe hang out with Connie and the other guests."

Jason chuckled. "Connie? Didn't Leona say she's high maintenance? Are you looking for someone handsome to keep her attention away from what you and Alex are doing?"

Annie jabbed Jason in the side with her elbow. "You know me too well. You have to admit that it's a solid plan, though, right? You talk to Connie, Alex and I chit chat with the other guests and try to find out what we can."

"You had me at come to the Blackbird for dinner. I don't mind being Connie's babysitter. I'll just ask her about herself and sit back and let her talk."

"Perfect." Annie swung her legs off the kitchen stool. "I'm off then. To what, I'm not sure so wish me luck."

Jason put his hand on Annie's arm. "Seriously, be careful. Someone there is a killer."

"Unless it's Robin's boyfriend, Jared, who is not there anymore. He went home. He's the only one who was upstairs the whole time, but what would be his motive?"

Jason shrugged. "Drugs? Money? In the wrong place at the wrong time? It might not be something premeditated."

"But Alex said the chef had a problem with someone. That certainly sounds like at least one person had it in for him. It seems highly unlikely that it would be Jared." Annie zipped her coat and grabbed her bag.

"What if Jared got caught in the chef's room, killed him, maybe accidentally, he panicked, and was afraid to admit what happened? That would mean that someone else was really after the chef in the first place. And don't forget, Annie, *someone* killed the other guy who was supposed to be at the Blackbird. Maybe that person was planning to kill the chef, too, but didn't have to since someone else got to him first. That means the killer could be relaxing and waiting for the opportunity to disappear from Catfish Cove."

"So, what you're telling me is that anything is possible. With two potential killers out there, finding the chef's murderer won't solve both crimes."

"Exactly." He blew her a kiss. "See you later."

"Come on, Roxy. Time to do something, not sure what, but one thing I can count on is that today will probably be filled with unexpected surprises."

As Annie drove to the Blackbird, she wondered about Alex and if he'd told her the whole truth. She assumed it was true that he was a private investigator because Jason checked on that. What she wouldn't be able to verify was whether Chef Marcel had in fact hired him or if Alex was investigating for someone else. He could have a partner who took care of Phil while *his* part of the scheme was to finish off the chef. But why?

The why was always the tricky part to figure out. *If* Phil and the chef were partners like Alex suggested, but Phil was pretending to be a workshop participant, it made sense to assume that they had some kind of scheme going. Or why else the deception? It would be easy to do some searches on the internet to find out what the chef's background was, what other workshops he ran, and maybe even find out who had gone to those other workshops. Did the chef not deliver what he promised?

Annie turned into the Blackbird's driveway and was disappointed to see the police chief's cruiser parked right up close. Bumping into Tyler first thing was not what she'd hoped for. She parked out of the way. Maybe she and Roxy could make a dash into Danny's workshop and avoid Tyler all together.

It was a good idea until the front door opened and Tyler walked briskly off the front porch. Right into Annie's escape route.

"Good morning, Tyler," Annie said pleasantly. She kept walking in the hopes that Tyler would do the same right past her to his cruiser.

He didn't.

"Annie." His tone made her stop. "I should have told you about Camilla and me."

"Listen, Tyler, it's okay. Camilla's great." She fiddled with the scarf around her neck. "It was just a shock at first. I only hope she will still hang out with *me* sometimes." Annie smiled.

"Why wouldn't she?"

Annie looked down while she dug the toe of her boot into the snow. "She's afraid she might spill something to me that she's not supposed to. You know, some police business."

"That's ridiculous. I don't talk about anything that hasn't been released already. That would be completely unprofessional."

"Good. Tell her so she doesn't turn into a jumpy mess whenever she sees me."

Tyler grinned. "She is kind of high strung, isn't she? Always bubbly and chatty; refreshing like the first bite into a lemon square. I love her spontaneity."

"Camilla is one of a kind," Annie said. "I truly hope this works out for both of you."

"You don't think it will?"

Annie didn't miss the concern in Tyler's voice. She should have kept her last comment to herself. "I didn't say that, Tyler. Don't be such a worrywart. Relax. Have some fun. You deserve it." She started to walk toward the front door.

"Before you go inside, Annie—" Tyler's voice changed to his no-nonsense police tone.

She stopped and turned back toward him, waiting . . . dreading what might be coming next.

"I know how you always manage to get involved when there's a murder here in Catfish Cove."

She held her breath, wondering where this was going.

"Don't do anything stupid. With one, or possibly two, killers on the loose, I don't want to be investigating any more deaths. Understand?" He lowered his head so he was looking at her over the top of his sunglasses.

And there it was, Tyler's condescending attitude that always scraped across Annie's skin like a knife grating on a plate. She cringed. "What are you suggesting, Tyler? That I shouldn't help

Leona get her bed and breakfast back on a normal footing? That I shouldn't even talk to any of the guests because one of them could be a killer? If you do your job I won't *be able* to get involved." She turned and stomped inside, slamming the door for good measure. Why did he always feel the need to say the obvious? And just when she thought they'd moved onto a new level with their friendship, he had to ruin it with his bossy attitude.

Buddy dashed toward Roxy and Annie on his short legs. That forced all frustration about Tyler from her mind as the two dogs sniffed, wagged, and said their doggy hellos. If only it was so easy with people. Annie sighed and followed the delicious smells into the kitchen.

Leona had her radio on her favorite oldies station but the volume was turned low. At the Black Cat Café she would blast it until opening time, but here she must have felt she had to keep the sound down out of respect for her guests.

"I'm looking forward to today," Leona said. "The sun is shining, I'll be baking all day," she turned away from the stove to look at Annie, "nothing more could possibly go wrong, right?"

Wrong, Annie said to herself. "Sure," she said to Leona. "What's the plan for today?"

Connie pushed through the door before Leona had a chance to answer. "Can I bother you for some more coffee?"

"A fresh pot is brewing, it will be ready before you can eat one of these fresh-from-the-oven blueberry muffins," Leona said as she handed a plate to Connie.

"Oh my." Connie patted her not-too-slim middle. "I'll need a whole new wardrobe when I get home with all the amazing baked goods you always have on hand." She took the plate. "You aren't working at the Black Cat Café today, Annie?"

"No, I'll be here as Leona's assistant for whatever she has planned." Annie helped herself to a warm muffin.

"I can't wait to get started. Will we be making éclairs still, like Chef Marcel had planned?"

"No, I'd rather stick with what I know best." She handed Connie a clean cup. "The coffee's ready."

"Oh, thanks. I guess you want me out of the way." Connie laughed. "One other question," she added as she filled her cup. "I can't find Buddy's favorite leash—it's blue, decorated with dog bones. I know this sounds silly but he doesn't like the one I have for a backup."

"We'll keep our eyes open for it. I'm sure it will turn up." Annie opened the kitchen door, hoping Connie got the message to leave.

She did, along with her coffee and a second blueberry muffin.

"I bumped into Tyler when I arrived. What was he doing here this morning?" Annie washed the muffin pan and Leona wiped all the work surfaces.

"He checked the chef's room again but it's still off limits. And I think he had some additional questions for George and Sarah but I've been busy in here getting breakfast done and planning the cooking lessons. Oh, wait, there was one thing that was odd." Leona leaned on the counter. "He wanted to know exactly how Jared got in and where Alex spent his time after he arrived."

"Huh." That made the hairs on Annie's neck rise. Was Tyler focused on those two as the top suspects? Jared was in the wrong place at the wrong time as far as Annie was concerned.

But Alex presented a different scenario. He wasted no time making himself at home and becoming friendly in a brand-new setting. Was that so they put their guard down while he gained their trust? What was he really after?

17

By the time Leona had all the work spaces for her baking demonstration ready to go at ten o'clock, the guests were chomping at the bit with nervous energy.

At least one of them was anxious to begin baking.

Connie beamed brighter than the sunshine reflecting on the snow when Leona ushered them into the kitchen.

George grumbled that this wasn't what he'd paid for.

Sarah fluttered around like an injured bird.

Robin shrugged and said, "Whatever," whenever anyone tried to get her involved in a conversation.

Alex smiled and chose a frilly pink apron to wear.

Annie watched and wondered which one of these people might be Chef Marcel's murderer.

"Okay," Leona began. Five pairs of eyes focused on her at the table facing the work stations. "I thought we'd start with something fairly simple but super delicious and eye-catching."

Connie grinned with delight. "I'm already drooling in anticipation."

Robin rolled her eyes as she tapped something into her phone.

"You all have strawberries in front of you."

Connie helped herself to one of them. Juice dribbled down her chin after she stuffed the whole thing in her mouth.

Robin held up her phone. "Do you mind if I make a video your demonstration?"

Leona smiled. "Great idea, Robin. We're going to make chocolate covered strawberries. First, and I've already done this for you, the strawberries need to be absolutely dry or the chocolate won't stick as well. It's best to pat them gently after rinsing, then lay them on a clean dish towel until completely dry. Second, and this is a personal preference, is your chocolate selection. Today we're using a gourmet semi-sweet chocolate which Annie chopped into small pieces for me." Leona held up a small bowl of chocolate bits.

"I don't have any chocolate," George complained.

"Right. Annie is melting enough chocolate for everyone. Once it's ready, you'll all get a bowl for dipping."

"This is a great gift idea," Sarah said as she looked at everyone else. "Right?"

"Yes, Sarah. That's what I was going to add. They are simple to make and the melt-in-your-mouth chocolate covering the sweet strawberry is impossible to resist."

Annie poured melted chocolate into the individual bowls for each person.

"What I do, when I'm making a lot, is have the pan lined with parchment paper on my right." Leona tilted her pan to show the others. "Now, grasp a strawberry by the leaves, dip and swirl in the chocolate to coat, gently shake off the excess, and lay it on the baking sheet." Leona demonstrated her technique as she explained the process. "Easy peasy. Your turn."

Annie walked around to offer help if needed. George dropped his strawberry in the chocolate. Connie licked the extra chocolate off her fingers. Sarah dipped her strawberry carefully but only got it half-way covered with chocolate. Alex executed a perfect chocolate covered strawberry. Robin filmed everyone with her phone.

The kitchen was surprisingly quiet as everyone concentrated on creating their masterpieces. Leona's tray filled quickly and she slid it in the refrigerator to cool for the last step.

After many dropped strawberries, dripped chocolate, and sticky fingers, everyone managed to create a few beautiful chocolate covered strawberries, and many messy ones.

"That was fun," Connie announced after she dropped her last berry on her tray. "When can we eat one?" the chocolate smear on her chin revealed that she had sampled hers already.

"The chocolate needs to set and then we can drizzle white chocolate on top if you want, for a fancier presentation. We'll eat them later."

Leona wiped her brow with the back of her hand. Annie could tell that this lesson had drained her even though it was a relatively easy project. She wondered what other baking ideas Leona had planned for the afternoon or if she would abandon the whole idea.

Annie heard scratching on the kitchen door. "I'll take the dogs out for a few minutes."

Alex wiped his hands on his frilly apron. "I don't mind helping with clean-up."

Leona sent him a silent thank you that Annie sensed before she turned her back.

Everyone else washed up and headed into the living room.

"I guess that wasn't so bad," Annie heard George say to Sarah as they left the kitchen. "At least we didn't have to listen to the chef's ridiculous fake accent."

That caught Annie's attention. Chef Marcel wasn't really French? She hadn't considered that possibility, which reminded her that she had planned to do some research on his background. She sent a text to Jason and asked him to do that since she didn't have time at the moment. As she got her boots on, Jason replied that he'd get right on it.

Roxy, with Buddy close behind, dashed through the door into the sunshine. Annie took a deep cleansing breath as she enjoyed watching the dogs frolic in the snow. Well, Roxy frolicked and Buddy disappeared. Annie laughed.

"He's a funny guy," Danny said as he headed toward Annie. "How's it going inside? Thanks for coming today to help; I was just getting in Leona's way."

"You gave her that break last night which she desperately needed. How was it being here by yourself with the guests?"

"Okay, I guess. That Robin is an odd one. She kept asking if she could take a picture of the chef's room. Why would she want to do that?"

Annie shook her head. "She's writing a novel, so who knows what information she'll find useful. She just filmed Leona's whole lesson. Maybe she thinks she can solve this crime? I don't know."

"Or she committed the crime," Danny said. "She could have, right?"

"Any one of them had the opportunity to sneak into the chef's room and kill him, but why? Plus, Robin's boyfriend who snuck in here Friday night is a suspect, too. He had a nervous twitch and shifty eyes that made him look guilty of *something*."

Danny pointed to a black Dodge Charger pulling into the driveway. "Company's coming."

"Oh, great. This I could do without," Annie said as Detective Crank parked in the spot where Tyler had been earlier. "I wonder what she's after now."

Christy took her time getting out of her car. She carried a notebook, camera, and a plastic bag. "Nice day," she said to Annie and Danny.

Buddy rushed over, barking ferociously.

Christy bent down. "Forgot me already?" She held her hand out, Buddy sniffed, wagged his tail, jumped, and licked Christy from chin to forehead. "Eww." She stood and wiped the dog slime off her face. "Not again. I thought we worked that out on Friday." She laughed as she wagged her finger at the dog.

Annie watched the interaction patiently, glad that Christy tolerated nonsense from dogs even if she didn't from their two-legged owners. "How is your investigation going?" The words flopped out without an expectation of a response.

"Great. That's exactly why I'm here. Another poke around for the murder weapon."

"Oh?"

Christy crouched and patted Buddy. "Does this little guy have a leash?"

"Connie has a whole wardrobe for him." Something clicked in Annie's mind. Connie said she couldn't find Buddy's leash. Annie stuck her hands in her coat pockets.

"I'm sure she does, but I'm only interested in his leash. Anyone traveling with a dog would have a leash," Christy stated.

Annie's hand slowly came out of her pocket. A blue leash with dog bone designs dangled from her fingers. "I forgot I tucked this in my pocket Friday night when I took the dogs out. It's Buddy's favorite leash. Connie said it went missing." Annie turned the leash over in her hand. Dog hairs were embedded on the underside.

"I'll bet she did." Christy's voice hardened. "Where is Connie?"

Christy reached for the leash. Annie gave it to her.

"Inside. Leona just finished a chocolate covered strawberry demonstration and now she's getting lunch ready. The guests were waiting in the living room."

"Good. I'll find her." Christy, with her no-nonsense stride, went to the kitchen door and let herself in.

"What was that all about?" Danny asked.

"I'm not one hundred percent certain, but my best guess is that Detective Crank suspects that leash is the murder weapon."

"A dog leash? The chef was strangled?"

"He drank a lot of wine so it might not have been too difficult to finish him off. But Connie? She doesn't seem like a murderer. She's friendly, chatty, and always in a good mood. Besides, what could she have against the chef?"

"Maybe it *wasn't* Connie. Someone might have taken the leash from her room," Danny suggested.

"I think that's a strong possibility." Annie's mind swirled. "Connie was one of the last people to go upstairs. Jared was upstairs the longest and then Alex went up not long after he arrived. Either of them could have gone into her room. George and Sarah went up before Connie and the chef so they would have had time, too."

"So, it doesn't really narrow anything down, does it?"

"Except that I helped Connie to her room after she passed out from the wine and heat. She fell asleep as soon as she landed on her bed. I would say she wasn't in any shape to murder anyone."

"Well, that's one less suspect," Danny said. "Who would have taken the leash?"

"Good question that I don't have an answer for."

Lunch was on the table by the time Annie and Danny took the dogs inside. She looked at everyone with new eyes.

Annie wondered, *who* could strangle someone and, more importantly, *why* would they?

18

Leona had a beautiful meal on the table—lasagna, a big bowl of Caesar salad, garlic bread, and a plate of chocolate covered strawberries. She pulled Annie away from the table and back into the kitchen.

"What's going on?" Leona hissed. "Christy came in all puffed up and strutting like a peacock. Did she talk to you outside?"

"Unfortunately, I did bump into her. It's not what we talked about though, as much as what I found in my pocket—Buddy's missing leash."

"Big deal. Did you tell Connie?" Then Leona's mouth formed into an O as she figured out the significance. She glanced around, checking to be sure they were alone. "It's connected to the chef's murder?" she whispered.

"I think so. At least, that's how Christy acted."

"How did it get in *your* pocket?"

"I must have shoved it in there Friday night when I took the dogs out. Remember? When Connie got Buddy's sweater and booties. I never hooked him up to the leash because, really, where was he going to go on those short legs during the snowstorm?"

Leona cracked the kitchen door leading into the dining room

and peeked through before she asked her next question. "Christy thinks Connie is the killer?"

"I have no idea what Christy is thinking but when I pulled that leash out of my pocket, she had a grin like she'd just opened a box full of gooey chocolate brownies. There must have been some reason they were looking for a dog leash."

The door from the dining room swung toward them, knocking into Leona's back. She spun around.

"Just who I was looking for. Do you mind if I help myself to some of your lunch spread?" Detective Crank asked. "I'm not sure your guests have much of an appetite and it would be a shame for that delicious food to go to waste."

Leona looked at Annie but no words came out.

Annie handed Christy a plate. "Help yourself but I hope you aren't planning to sit at the table with the guests. There's a table in here."

Christy frowned. "I don't want to be rude. I'll sit in the dining room." Christy disappeared into the dining room.

"We'd better get out there too before, well, I don't know what might happen with her sitting with everyone," Leona said. She handed Annie a pitcher of ice water and she carried a fresh pot of coffee. "Ready to run some interference?"

"I'll do my best. At least we'll be able to hear any conversation first hand but I'm afraid I just lost my appetite." The thought of Leona's cooking normally made Annie's stomach grumble but at the moment she was too stressed to eat.

As the door opened, the first sight that met Annie was Connie's white face and frightened eyes. "Yes. That's Buddy's leash," she mumbled. "Why do you have it?"

Detective Crank, who was holding a plastic evidence bag with the leash inside for all to see, sat opposite Connie. "Was this in your room before the chef was found dead?"

"I, um, I'm not sure. I'll have to think back. When are you asking me about?" Connie's eyes blinked rapidly.

Detective Crank put the evidence bag on her lap. She took a big forkful of lasagna. Chewed. Swallowed. Tension escalated in the room. "Friday, Ms. Cook. The first day of the workshop. The day of the snowstorm. The day of the power outage. The day Chef Marcel was killed. I can't make it any clearer than that. So, let me ask you again. Was this leash in your room on Friday?"

"I suppose it was at least some of the time."

"Some of the time," Christy repeated. She barely tried to hide her annoyance.

Annie and Leona took the two empty chairs at the table. Annie sat next to Robin and Leona sat next to Alex.

"Um," Connie swallowed and started again. "You see, Detective Crank. I wasn't in my room that whole time so how can I know if someone took the leash out?"

A grin spread on the detective's face. "Clever answer, but who do you think might have taken it out of your room?" Christy helped herself to several chocolate covered strawberries even though she hadn't finished her lasagna or salad.

"Well, I don't know." Connie looked around the table, stopping when she faced Robin. "I suppose anyone here *could* have gone in my room. I didn't lock the door. If I recall correctly, Robin's boyfriend was in her room hiding and *she* went up before the rest of us." Her head swiveled to look at Alex who sat next to her. "And Alex went upstairs soon after he arrived."

"It might help if you can remember when you last used the leash to take Buddy outside," Annie prompted.

Christy glared at her.

Annie continued anyway, turning away from Christy's stare. "Did you take Buddy out when you arrived here at the Blackbird? I would expect he might have needed a quick walk before you went in or maybe after you let Leona know you'd arrived."

Connie smiled. She pointed her finger at Annie. "You are brilliant. Of course, that's what happened. I went inside and dropped my bags near the stairs and let Leona know I'd made it safely.

The roads were already pretty bad by then. I did take Buddy out but, with the snow, I didn't bother with his leash which I looped on the coat tree near the door." She took a chocolate covered strawberry and popped it in her mouth. She had a self-satisfied look that must have meant she'd wiggled out of that awkward situation somewhat gracefully.

"Okay," Christy said. Annie could tell she was putting this all together. "The leash ended up in your pocket, Annie. Did you take it off the coat tree?"

Interesting question, Annie thought. Where did Connie get the leash when she brought Buddy's outside paraphernalia for Annie to take the dog out on Friday? "No. Connie gave me the leash, along with Buddy's other outside gear."

Christy's eyebrows jerked up. "Other outside gear?"

"Yeah. His sweater and booties. I didn't use the leash and must have shoved it in my pocket and forgot about it with all the stuff going on that night."

Christy jotted some notes in her little black notebook before she asked her next question. "Connie. Where did you find the leash when you gave all of Buddy's gear to Annie? Was it still on the coat tree?"

Connie stopped chewing her strawberry. It made a big lump in her cheek. She closed her eyes. "I never went to the coat tree. I went upstairs." She opened her eyes but she wasn't looking at anyone in particular, it was more like she was reliving her actions from Friday night as she finished her strawberry. "Buddy's gear bag was on my bed and I chose his red and black sweater with the matching red booties. I didn't take the red leash which matches better because he prefers the blue one but I couldn't find it in the bag so I dumped everything out on my bed. One of his toys fell off and rolled across the room, stopping when it hit the blue leash coiled at one side of the door. You know," she focused on Annie, "it was odd that it was there, but I didn't think about it at the time because you were waiting downstairs and I wanted to sit by the fire again to warm up. The power was still off and it was cold upstairs."

Christy jotted more notes. She looked at Annie. "Who else was upstairs then?"

"I don't remember but everyone had been upstairs before dinner when the power went out."

"So, anyone here could have taken the leash off the coat tree, taken it upstairs, and tossed it in Connie's room before dinner."

Annie nodded. "Anyone here plus Robin's boyfriend, Jared. He was hiding upstairs. Leona and I didn't find him until after we discovered the chef was dead."

Christy slapped her notebook closed and tucked it in her shirt pocket. She nibbled on one end of a strawberry, getting more chocolate than fruit with her taste. She waved the treat at Leona. "So delicious." She pushed herself back from the table and stood. "I hate to leave this lovely gathering but there's work to be done."

"Well, who did it?" Connie blurted out.

Christy grinned. "You'll be the first to know," she said before she let herself out.

"What's that supposed to mean?" Connie asked. "The first to know? Does she think *I* murdered the chef?"

Sarah, who had been sitting next to Connie, patted her arm. "I'm sure that's not it. You were helpful and she just meant she'd let you know when she figures it all out. I think it was that boy hiding upstairs."

"Don't look at me," Robin said. "If Jared killed the chef, he certainly didn't confide in me." She got up from the table and silently disappeared.

"She's like a ghost, and what is she always doing with that phone of hers?" Sarah asked. "Maybe *she's* the murderer," she added as an afterthought.

Maybe, Annie thought. She looked carefully at each of the guests at the table—Sarah, quiet and timid; Connie, outspoken and friendly; Alex, helpful with a touch of mystery; and George, sullen and angry. Jared nervously hightailed it home, which made him look guilty of *something*.

Which brought her thoughts back to Robin and how she said *she* knew who killed the chef. Did she mean she knew who kill him in her novel or did *she* do it and was trying to divert the focus to everyone else? The number of possible murderers was stuck at six.

nnie carried a stack of plates into the kitchen. Leona followed close behind.

"This all has me completely creeped out." Leona set a pan still half-filled with lasagna on the counter. "By the looks of what *wasn't* eaten, I think Christy's presence had a chilling effect on the guests' appetites."

"I saw Christy leave and figured it was safe to come inside," Danny sheepishly said as he entered the kitchen from the back door and threw his red baseball cap on the table. "What happened? I just caught your last comment." He eyed the lasagna and grabbed a plate. "Are you saving this for anything?"

"No. Help yourself. There's salad, too." Leona left the kitchen and returned with more leftovers. "It seems someone took a fancy to the chocolate covered strawberries. Every last one has disappeared; along with all the guests."

Danny cut himself a hefty serving of lasagna and slid it on his plate. He tipped the rest of the salad next to his portion. "So, anything new?"

"Not really," Annie said thoughtfully. "Except that Christy might be focused on Connie because of the dog leash."

"Buddy's leash?" Danny's forehead scrunched in confusion.

"Christy didn't *say* the leash was the murder weapon, but she sure was excited when I pulled it out of my pocket."

Danny sat at the kitchen table. "Maybe there were dog hairs on the chef's neck." He took a big bite of lasagna. "Mmmm," he mumbled, "delicious."

Annie looked at Leona. "Of course!" It was like a lightbulb went off. "Dog hairs could connect the leash to the chef. Why didn't one of us think of that?"

"You two make everything too complicated," Danny said. "Me? I'm just a simple carpenter." He continued eating and grinning. "Glad I could be of some help before I have to leave."

"What's your plan for the afternoon?" Annie asked Leona.

Leona's gaze traveled around the kitchen. "Cleanup is first on my list, then round two of my workshop. Why? You aren't thinking of bailing out on me, are you?"

"Could you do without me for an hour or so?" Annie fidgeted.

Leona, who had started rinsing dishes and filling the dishwasher, turned to look at Annie. "I'm not sure I like the sound of your question. What are you planning?"

"I want to go to Bigger Burger and ask a few questions. Chef Marcel and Phil were there on Friday according to my neighbor's son. Maybe someone who works there heard something or saw something. If he hasn't told the police yet, Christy won't have followed that thread."

"I don't know," Leona waffled.

"I have time to help you clean up before I leave," Danny offered. "If Annie leaves now, she'll be back before you have a chance to miss her."

"Okay. But be back by three. I'll need your help with the next project—my cherry cake. I have to do *something* with all the cherries Chef Marcel left here. I wish he had left his recipes, too."

"Sure, no problem." Annie was already halfway out of the

kitchen. She wasn't going to dawdle and give Leona a chance to change her mind.

On her way through the living room, she found Roxy curled up on the couch next to Connie and Buddy. Connie's head was tipped to one side, her mouth hanging open and soft snoring noises coming out with each breath. Roxy perked up. Annie patted her leg and Roxy followed.

Once outside, Annie sent a text to Jason saying she was stopping at the house and for him to be ready for an outing. She didn't explain anything else, there would be time for that when he joined her. Besides, her plan was simple—see if anyone at Bigger Burger remembered any morsel of information about Chef Marcel. If yes, she'd figure out what to ask.

Leaving Roxy at home with the cats, Annie and Jason headed out with Jason behind the wheel. "This is a surprise," he said. "You're sneaking out to a restaurant instead of eating Leona's food?"

"Not exactly. When Christy showed up at lunchtime and sat at the table with the guests, I lost my appetite. It's back now, though." She grinned and patted her stomach. "Did you discover anything of interest in Chef Marcel's background?" Annie asked as Jason drove through Catfish Cove.

"Sort of, but it was conflicting. You know how people can be online when they post reviews about stuff?"

Annie nodded.

"Well, I found a couple of scathing reviews by extremely dissatisfied participants in one of his workshops last year."

"Different people?"

"As far as I could tell. The complaint was that Chef Marcel had no clue what he was doing and relied on his assistant to more or less run the demonstration instead of doing everything himself."

"An assistant? Let me guess, was his name Phil?"

"Close enough. In the review, he was referred to as Philip. Do you suppose it's the same Phil who turned up dead on Friday?" Jason pulled into the parking lot of Bigger Burger.

"Yes, I definitely suppose that's possible. Did you find out anything about this Philip?"

"Possibly." Jason grinned.

Annie twisted in the seat to face Jason. "Tell me before I explode."

"An unnamed participant shared what he overheard Philip and Chef Marcel arguing about."

"No kidding. How did you find *that*?"

"When I Googled the chef's name," Jason turned the car off, "I found an article by a food critic who was doing a segment on one of the workshops. He included an interview with Chef Marcel, who did a great job promoting himself. But he also interviewed this unnamed person who painted a different picture— unhappy participants, demands for refunds, and the rumor of a scam in the works."

"Oh, some juicy gossip? That's great."

"That's for sure. The article went on with more comments about the chef and it wasn't all flattery."

"Interesting. Wouldn't the people who came to the Blackbird look up reviews before signing up for one of these workshops?"

"You would think so, but, apparently, some people are just too trusting. And there's that whole," Jason used his fingers to make air quotes, "*French Chef mystique.*"

"But," Annie felt some excitement brewing inside, "I bet someone who came to the Blackbird knew some of the chef's history and that's why he's dead now—revenge."

"But what about Phil? Do you know how he died?"

"Poison is the rumor going around. With a bit of luck we're getting closer to more detail if someone inside Bigger Burger has any information." Annie opened the car door and stepped out. She was glad to see that there weren't many cars in the parking lot which meant whoever was working might find time for a friendly chat.

"I printed these for you, too." Jason handed Annie a couple of folded papers.

When she opened them, she smiled. "Good thinking." One page was a photo of Chef Marcel and the other was a photo of a Philip Hanks.

Annie opened the restaurant door and walked inside. A sleigh bell announced them. It was a small but cozy space. The menu was printed on a big blackboard above the counter—a big selection of burgers, pizzas, drinks, and fries. Half a dozen tables were available but, at the moment, no patrons were sitting. One man finished paying and left with two bags of food. The smells were mouthwatering.

Annie and Jason studied the menu before approaching the counter.

"How are you doing today?" Annie said with a smile at the waitress.

"Okay." She pushed some stray hairs away from her face and held her pencil ready. "Ready to order?"

"Um, I'll have your veggie burger with caramelized onions and cheddar cheese," Jason said, then left and sat at one of the small tables for two.

"The bacon cheeseburger for me, please." Annie smiled and was glad to see that the woman's uniform had a name tag pinned on the breast pocket.

"To go?" the thirtyish woman asked.

"Not today. We'll eat here, Tricia."

Tricia smiled. "Thanks for noticing." She called the order to the cook standing at the grill and turned back toward Annie. "Is there something else?"

"Two waters . . . and I'm wondering if you were working last Friday afternoon."

Tricia rolled her eyes toward the ceiling as if she was looking back in time. "I was. Why?"

Annie held up the two photos. "Do you recognize either of these guys?"

Tricia's eyes opened wide. "Are you a cop or something?"

"No." Annie had to think up a convincing story. "This one," she pointed to the chef's photo, "was running a pastry workshop at my aunt's Blackbird Bed and Breakfast and we're all just devastated about what happened."

"What do you mean?" Tricia's eyes narrowed.

"You didn't hear? Well, this one," she held up Phil's photo, "died sometime between when he was here and before he arrived at the Blackbird. The chef died," Annie lowered her voice, "right in his room at the bed and breakfast. In bed." Annie grimaced.

Tricia's hand covered her mouth. "That's terrible."

"Do you remember seeing them here?"

Tricia looked around and leaned toward Annie. "I served them but my boss," she nodded her head toward the cook, "doesn't want me talking about it. Bad for business, he said."

"Oh, I understand completely. That's why I'm trying to figure out what happened—you know, to help my aunt out with her business." Annie tilted her head, raised her eyebrows and gave Tricia what she hoped was her best please-help-me-out-here look.

Tricia looked at her watch. She whispered. "I'm off in a half hour. After you eat, we could talk somewhere else."

Annie smiled and nodded. She reached her hand out and patted Tricia's arm. "Thank you."

Annie returned to the table and sat across from Jason. "Did you work your pleading puppy dog eyes on the waitress to get her talking?"

"I did. She agreed to talk to me after we eat and her shift is done. Her boss doesn't want any bad publicity for his business."

Jason sat with his elbow resting on the table and his hand

cupped around one side of his mouth. "Something must have happened if he's nervous about bad publicity. Usually, any publicity is good but I suppose when it comes to murder, people might freak out and avoid this place."

Annie nodded but she was already thinking about something else. "A couple of things I heard make more sense now," Annie said. "Thelma's son said he heard Phil tell the chef to pay up or the whole deal was over, and you uncovered this article about unhappy customers and a possible scam. So—" her fingernails clicked on the wood table. She leaned closer to Jason. "I'm thinking that maybe Phil was blackmailing the chef."

Tricia appeared with two plates overflowing with food and two waters. "Here you go. One veggie burger and one bacon cheeseburger." She lowered her voice. "I added extra fries so if you take your time you'll be done when my shift ends."

"Thanks, Tricia." Annie laughed. "This is a mountain of food. I might need a doggy bag." Annie added a mound of ketchup to her plate and sampled a fry. "Hot and crispy, just the way I like them."

The restaurant door jingled. Jason, who faced the front door, said, "Don't look now." He nibbled on a fry.

Of course, Annie turned to look. She groaned.

Detective Crank *and* Police Chief Johnson headed to the counter. Tricia looked up, first at the two officers, then she caught Annie's eye.

"Where's your boss?" Christy leaned on the counter and looked around. She smirked when she saw Annie. Tyler kept his back to her.

With that attitude, Christy wouldn't get any information from Tricia's boss, Annie thought to herself. She didn't even take the time to learn Tricia's name. In another twenty minutes, Tricia would be talking to her instead of the police.

20

Detective Crank ambled over to Annie and Jason's table while the owner finished at the grill. She gave the illusion that the most important thing on her mind was a juicy burger. Annie knew otherwise.

"Nice place. Do you come here often?" Christy asked, but Annie didn't fail to understand the underlying question.

Annie finished her bite of burger. She could see Christy beginning to seethe with impatience. She wiped her mouth before she answered. "Occasionally, how about you? I highly recommend the bacon cheeseburger. It's juicy with the perfect complement of crispy bacon and cheese." Annie took another bite, knowing that wasn't the information Christy was after.

Christy put both hands on the table and stared at Annie. "What are you doing here?" she hissed between clenched teeth.

"Eating. Is that a problem?" Annie felt Jason bump her foot but she ignored his warning to stop giving cute answers. They both knew what was behind Christy's question.

"Why *here*, Annie? Why *here* where a murder victim was last seen alive?"

Annie's hand covered her mouth, just like Tricia had done

earlier. Only Annie's gesture was mock shock. "You're kidding." Annie pushed her plate away. "You think he died from this food?"

Christy pulled another chair to the small table and squeezed between Annie and Jason. "Your neighbor's son told me about the conversation he heard here Friday night between Chef Marcel and Phil Hanks. He told me *you* said he should share the information with me. So, let me ask you one more time—*why* are you here?"

Annie's eyes shifted to Tricia. Did she know anything? Annie looked at Christy and shrugged. "Curiosity. Leona is a mess because of the murder and I'm curious if anyone here heard anything. The sooner this is wrapped up, the better for her business."

"Agreed. Did you find out anything?" Christy's tone changed only slightly, letting Annie know that they were on the same side even if they couldn't work together.

Annie shook her head. Not yet since she hadn't talked with Tricia and she didn't feel the need to send Christy after the poor waitress who was jumpier than a rabbit trying to escape becoming dinner for some hungry fox.

Christy stood. "Two people are dead. Don't let it become three." She walked back to the counter where the owner was waiting for her.

Annie couldn't hear their conversation but she could see the man shake his head after every one of Christy's or Tyler's questions. If he knew anything, he wasn't sharing it with them.

Jason nudged Annie's foot with his. He tilted his head toward the exit. Tricia had just disappeared through the door.

"I have to catch her before she changes her mind and ditches me," Annie whispered. "I'll go out and you can get a doggie bag for the leftovers." She pulled her jacket on as she hustled toward the door. She didn't dare glance at Christy but hoped that she was still occupied with the owner and didn't notice her quick departure.

It was all in vain. All Annie saw as the door closed behind her was an older, rusty Honda leaving the parking lot. Tricia must have known something and that something had her spooked, was all Annie could imagine.

She heard the door open behind her and felt Jason's arm on her shoulder. "No luck?"

"I was too late. I'll have to swing by tomorrow and try to catch her if she's working then. Let's get out of here before Detective Crank comes out. I don't think the owner will share anything since he told Tricia not to talk to anyone. Besides, I promised Leona I'd be back to help her with her next baking session."

They walked to Jason's car. "What's she teaching next?"

"Cherry cake."

"That doesn't sound particularly interesting. To me at least. Do you want me to come with you now or wait until later?" Jason pulled out of the parking lot.

"We'll all be busy in the kitchen until at least four so come then if you want. Once the session is done, Leona will have to get dinner ready for the guests." Annie patted her stomach. "I won't be hungry after that burger."

"Okay. I'll plan on hanging out in the living room to keep the fireplace going and make friends with Connie or anyone else who comes in. Will that be helpful?"

Annie put her hand on Jason's thigh. "Extremely. Just ask a few innocent questions and see where the conversation goes. Connie loves to hear herself talk. If Robin says *anything*, it will have some sort of meaning since she chooses her words carefully. George sulks but, who knows, maybe he'll open up to another man. His wife, Sarah, just frets about everything."

"And Alex?"

"Oh yeah. I tend to forget about him since he wasn't one of the original participants. He has me stumped. You met him. How likely do you think it is that he could be the murderer?" Every instinct told Annie that Alex wasn't a killer but she had to be careful not to rule anyone out. And he had the odd timing to pop up when something was happening, which was disconcerting. Was that the private investigator side of him or was he trying to keep his finger on the pulse of what was happening to stay ahead of getting caught?

"You know, Annie, any one of the people who was stranded at the Blackbird could be the murderer." He gave her a serious look. "Don't forget it and let your emotions get in the way of logical thinking. That being said, how likely do I think it's Alex? Not very at this point. But, really, what motive do any of them have that we know of?"

Annie sighed. "It could have something to do with what you found in those reviews—an unhappy past participant."

"But murder? Why not just get a refund? And who killed the other guy?" Jason pulled into their driveway. "Want me to bring Roxy over later?"

"That's a good idea." Before Annie hopped out, she said, "I hope, once I find Tricia, she has some more clues to what happened to Phil and Chef Marcel last Friday. The way she high-tailed it from Bigger Burger when she got off work makes me think she's running away from talking about something she heard." She slid out of Jason's car and walked to hers.

"I'll see you around four," Jason said.

The Blackbird kitchen smelled mouthwateringly delicious when Annie walked in through the back door. Leona had a row of small cakes lined up on cooling racks.

"What's that?"

"Thank goodness you're back. I decided to make some cakes ahead of time in case you got sidetracked. This way we don't have to wait for the new batch to bake. I'll have everyone mix up batter and get their cakes in the oven, but then I can use these and get right to the frosting and decorating."

"It looks like you made a bunch of chocolate cakes. I thought you were teaching how to make a cherry cake." Annie bent down to smell one of the warm confections.

"I had to think of something a bit fancier so I dug out this different recipe. It's something I haven't made in a long time but I'm sure everyone will love it. It's an individual serving of my rich cherry buried cake. It's guaranteed to be a hit—layers of chocolate cake with cream cheese frosting and cherries between the layers, then it's all covered with chocolate ganache and more cherries." Leona licked her lips.

"The cherries go between the layers?"

"Some of them. There are several steps. I've got the dark chocolate ganache ready in this pot. The cream cheese filling is here, and I simmered some of the cherries with sugar and some cherry brandy. Fresh cherries will decorate the top after the layers are assembled." Leona's voice filled the kitchen with her excitement for her creation.

Alex poked his head into the kitchen. "Is it safe to come in yet?"

Leona nodded. "Get an apron and pick your spot. I won't get started until everyone is here, though."

Alex started to touch one of the individual cakes.

Leona swatted his hand away. "No touching! These are for after a new batch of batter is made and in the oven."

Alex grinned. "You drive a hard bargain, Leona. Just walking into your kitchen gets my salivary glands dancing a tango." He chose an apron covered with kitchen utensils this time—sharp knives being the main item. Odd choice, Annie thought.

Leona actually blushed a little from Alex's compliment. He had her twisted around his finger with his helpfulness and praise. Annie wasn't sure that was a good thing.

"I heard something interesting today about Chef Marcel," Annie said, changing the subject from mouthwatering yumminess to stomach-turning worries.

"Oh?" Alex gave her his undivided attention.

Leona scowled.

"Were you aware of some scathing reviews about one of his recent workshops?"

The edge of Alex's lip twitched as if he was making a decision on what he wanted to share with Annie. "Yes. I've been doing some searching online and came across something. If I knew who Chef Marcel had a problem with, it would be easier to make a connection to an actual person but, unfortunately, I never got that piece of information."

"And Phil, or Philip as he was referred to in an article, was the one actually running the demonstration."

"Yes, I saw that, too."

Annie sent Jason a silent congratulations on his expert sleuthing. "I have a theory."

Both Alex and Leona stared at Annie.

"I think there's a possibility that Phil was blackmailing the chef."

"Well," Leona said, "there's no way that Phil killed the chef. He was already dead. So, how does your theory help to solve anything?"

"What if it was the chef who killed Phil and someone here killed the chef for a completely different reason? I've been thinking about how the chef behaved before everyone went upstairs. He was flustered by everything—the storm, Phil not arriving, Alex showing up. Was he trying to find any excuse to get out of doing the workshop because he couldn't do it on his own? I guess, what I'm wondering is, was the chef a fraud?"

Leona's mouth fell open. "And I was worried about what he thought of *my* cooking?"

Alex nodded. "I've wondered that, too. But how could he have killed Phil? And why would he if it impacted his own performance?"

"The only thing that makes sense to me right now is that Phil was blackmailing the chef. If he killed Phil and somehow wiggled out of this workshop, he could regroup and find another person to help him. I found someone who might be able to shed more light on what went on at Bigger Burger."

Alex's mouth opened but closed as the kitchen door opened and the rest of the guests filed in. Annie let out a burst of air. This put an end to the speculation about Phil and Chef Marcel's murders. For now.

Leona moved straight into her teaching mode without missing a beat.

Alex stared at Annie. His gaze bore into her as if he was trying to read her mind. She could tell he was dying of curiosity to find out what she knew but she didn't plan to mention Tricia's name to him. She would wait until she found Tricia again to hear whatever she had to share.

21

Once Leona got the baking demonstration under way, everyone seemed to be able to forget about the murder investigation going on around them.

Connie dipped her finger in her cake batter like a naughty three-year-old. "Yum. I love chocolate. But how is this going to be a cherry cake?" She took one of the cherries in a bowl at her space, dipped it in the batter, and popped it in her mouth. "This is delicious."

Robin tried to swivel her phone to catch everyone's progress and comments. Her ingredients were untouched and no batter filled her bowl.

George meticulously measured and stirred, ignoring everyone else. He was focused but it was hard to tell if he was enjoying himself.

Sarah spilled half of her premeasured ingredients on the table. Annie chuckled when she tried to sneakily brush her table clean. Did she think her cake would come out properly with half of the ingredients on the floor?

Alex hummed, measured, and stirred. He was the only one

who seemed to be enjoying the baking lesson. Or was that just his cover?

A thumping on the front door caught Annie's attention. She looked at Leona who rolled her eyes. "Can you check who's there? It's probably Detective Crank again. She usually just barges in, though, and doesn't bother knocking."

Annie wiped her hands and pushed through the kitchen door. She was impressed with how well Leona had everything under control. Annie didn't feel like she was even needed in the kitchen at this point in the lesson. She pulled the front door open, wondering what rude comment would fall off Detective Crank's tongue; probably a follow-up question about why she was at Bigger Burger earlier.

"Can I come in?" Tricia's timid voice surprised Annie who pushed the door completely open and pulled Tricia toward her.

"Of course." Annie stepped to one side so Tricia could move completely inside. Annie closed the door before Tricia could change her mind and skitter away like a scared deer. "I was wondering how I would track you down. I certainly wasn't about to ask your boss for your contact information."

"Thank you for that." Tricia's voice trembled, still barely higher than a whisper of wind through the trees. "That's why I came here. I was terrified you'd ask him something about me." She looked around the big entryway. "Is there someplace private where we can talk?"

Annie led Tricia to the living room. With all the guests in the kitchen, she hoped they could talk undisturbed.

Tricia stood just inside the doorway. She wrapped her arms around herself even though it was toasty warm with the fireplace burning. "After you mentioned the Blackbird Bed and Breakfast I took a gamble hoping I'd find you here."

"You lucked out. Would you like some tea? Or coffee?" Annie wanted to help Tricia relax.

Tricia shook her head. "No. I just think someone should know what I remembered but I don't want to stay too long."

"Okay." Annie gently guided Tricia to one of the comfy chairs. She sat kitty corner to her guest, hoping that would be a bit less intrusive than facing her directly. "Go ahead whenever you're ready." She forced her body to remain still instead of showing her impatience.

Before Tricia worked up the courage to speak, footsteps sounded in the dining room. She looked at Annie with fear. What did she know? Tricia stood; her head turned one way then the other as she scanned for an intruder.

Alex poked his head into the living room. "Leona asked me to find out who was at the door."

Tricia quickly turned her face away from Alex.

Sensing Tricia's discomfort, Annie laughed and put herself between Alex and Tricia, drawing his attention to herself. "Tell Leona it's not the detective and I'll be right back to help."

Alex smiled. "The batter is in the oven and we are about to start assembling the final product. Just so you know." He waved and left.

"That guy," Tricia said when she was alone with Annie again, "who is he?"

"A private investigator. Why?" If fear had a scent, Annie was sure it was what she smelled near Tricia at the moment.

"Do you think he saw my face?"

"I don't know. He wasn't at the doorway for long." Annie stepped closer to Tricia. "What's got you so freaked out?"

"I saw him at Bigger Burger on Friday. He came in after those other two men but they didn't pay any attention to him. At the time, I didn't think too much of it, but considering what happened . . ."

"Listen, Tricia, you should go to the police. You could be the key to solving these murders."

Her face lost all color at those words. "I don't want to be

involved. My boss was right." She inched toward the door. "I don't know why I didn't listen to him. 'Don't say anything,' he told me. 'Don't get involved,' he insisted. Did I listen?" She looked into Annie's eyes with fear. "No. And now that guy saw me here. What if he comes after me next?"

Annie held Tricia's arm and gave it a little shake. "Why do you think that?"

"He got his coffee and sat at a corner table with his back to those two guys. I thought he was reading something on his phone when I brought his burger, but he was watching them. He must have had his camera on reverse. I could see the image of both men clearly on his phone."

"Did he talk to them?"

Tricia shook her head. "I don't think so. I thought it was all strange but it's not my job to monitor what customers are doing. It's only after they turned up dead that I thought it might mean something. And that guy is here where you told me one of the guys was murdered. It can't all be a coincidence."

By now, Annie could feel Tricia trembling under her hand. "What else happened?"

"Nothing," she mumbled and looked away from Annie.

"You came here to tell me something and that was before you knew Alex would be here. Tell me, Tricia."

She hesitated but it was obvious she wanted to get something off her conscience. "The guy with the mustache?"

"The chef?"

"I don't know. The other one called him Marcel." Her voice was so soft Annie had to move within inches of Tricia's mouth. "He came to the counter and asked for a cappuccino which is why I remember the order. We only serve regular coffee, nothing fancy. He wasn't too happy about that but he said 'Fine.' Then he took a container out of his pocket—some kind of prescription bottle—and dumped something into the coffee. He had moved off to the side but I saw it out of the corner of my eye. Do you think it could be important?"

"Why?" Annie didn't see anything wrong. If Chef Marcel was taking a prescription that didn't taste good, adding it to his drink made sense.

Tricia paused. "Because he gave the coffee to the other guy. I heard him say it was hot so save it for later. He also said not to follow him right away, or something like that."

What did Chef Marcel dump in the coffee? If it was a prescription, where was the bottle?

"I've got to go. Please don't tell anyone you got this information from me. I've got kids. I need my job. Don't tell the police I talked to you." Tricia's eyes pleaded with Annie to protect her before she pulled away from her grasp and darted out the door.

Annie stood and looked at the closed door. What did it all mean? Did the chef kill Phil to get out from under something? Blackmail? Was he going to ruin the chef's profitable pastry workshops and soon-to-be-released cookbook? Or was it all just a scam and he could feel it all closing in on him? Too many questions swirled in Annie's head.

The door opened, almost knocking into Annie.

"Are you okay?" Roxy rushed inside to find Buddy. Jason hung up his coat. "I saw Tricia get into her car as I pulled in. What happened?"

"She's about as jumpy as anyone I've ever seen." Annie took a quick check behind her to be sure they were alone. "She saw Alex at Bigger Burger on Friday. He was watching Phil and Chef Marcel."

"He could have just been doing his job, Annie; you know, keeping an eye on the chef to make sure he was safe."

"Maybe. But be careful around him just in case. The whole thing really unnerved Tricia. Plus—"

"There's more?"

"Tricia saw Chef Marcel dump something into a coffee he bought for Phil. She said it was from a prescription bottle."

"You think the chef poisoned Phil?"

Annie nodded.

"You have to tell Detective Crank this information."

"I know, but poor Tricia is afraid she'll lose her job if her boss finds out she talked to me. Coming here was risky enough for her and she refuses to talk to the police. I don't want her to get in trouble."

"Maybe Alex saw it all, too. Get *him* to tell the police."

"I'll think about it. But I'd better get back in the kitchen to help Leona with the rest of her demonstration."

"I'll take the dogs out and hang out in the living room when I come back in. Send all the guests my way if you want." Jason put his coat back on and called the two dogs. They barreled toward the door, almost sliding into it before Jason got it open. Roxy ran in circles chasing her own tail and Buddy barked encouragement. Finally, the door opened and Jason followed the two rambunctious dogs outside.

Annie took a deep breath before she entered the kitchen.

Alex was the first to look up from his beautifully frosted cake after he plopped a fresh cherry on top.

Annie couldn't quite read his expression. Was it simply curiosity or something more sinister?

22

T he top layer of Connie's cake slid off the bottom and landed on its edge. "Oh dear. I just can't get the hang of this." She pushed the layer back into place, licked the chocolate ganache frosting off her fingers, and watched as it slid off the other side in slow motion.

Annie went to the rescue after seeing Leona's look of desperation. Patience with someone who showed no baking talent was *not* Leona's forte.

"I think you have too much filling between the layers. Here, let's scrape some off." Annie handed Connie a blunt knife.

Connie did what Annie suggested. Then she licked the knife. "This is delicious. Even if I can't get it too look as nice as it's supposed to, it still tastes amazing." She broke off a chunk of the top layer and ate that, too.

Robin filmed the whole process as she walked around the kitchen, stopping at each work station. She showed more interest in the process than the product. She even took time to focus on the ingredients in their various stages of production.

"What's this?" Robin pointed to a bowl next to the sink.

Leona turned her head to see what Robin was asking about. "Oh, that's going in the compost."

"But what is it?"

"All the cherry pits. I wanted to save all of you from that tedious job so I pitted all the cherries we're using."

Robin picked up a pit. "Did you know," she seemed to be talking more to herself than the others in the room, "that these are harmless if swallowed whole . . . but a few crushed cherry pits could kill someone."

Annie's head jerked up, as did Alex's, but everyone else was too focused on keeping their cake from sliding apart and ending up on the floor to pay much attention to Robin.

"How do you even know that?" Annie asked. Robin's words made her stomach lurch. It was the second time she had mentioned killing someone with poison.

Robin flicked her free hand as if to indicate she thought Annie's question was about as dumb as could be. "Research, of course," she replied with an eye roll that so many young adults had perfected in their teenage years. "I've made a list of ways a person could kill someone for my novel. You know, research is important to get the little details correct."

Annie was sure she heard an almost soundless *duh* follow her answer. And she did agree with Robin about research getting the details correct, but did she need the details for her novel *or* for a real-life murder? Annie wondered. What could Robin's motive be if she was involved with Phil's or Chef Marcel's murders? Unless she wanted to experience her murder method for a more accurate description. That was just too gruesome to be a possibility.

Robin continued her rounds through the kitchen, stopping next at George's creation. "Not bad for a beginner."

George had managed to make a passable cake. He wiped his forehead with the back of his hand. "This is harder than it looks." He looked at Sarah's cake and frowned. "You aren't being careful enough," he scolded her.

Sarah's cake was all in one piece, unlike Connie's, but one side was much higher than the other. And she had the whole top covered with cherries instead of just a few for decoration.

The cake in front of Alex mirrored Leona's the closest—symmetrical, smooth ganache, and a few cherries artfully placed on top. "What do you think?" he asked Annie when he caught her eye.

She had no choice but to join him at his spot. "I'd say you've done some baking in a past life. Am I correct?"

Alex moved close to Annie. "You're very observant." He lowered his voice so only Annie could hear. "What did the waitress come here for?"

Annie's skin crawled at the question. How would she keep Tricia safe? "What were you doing at Bigger Burger?" A question for a question was safer than providing an answer to his curiosity.

Alex nodded his head toward the door. Annie followed him out of the kitchen.

"It could be dangerous for her to come here but I don't think anyone saw her but me," Alex said as soon as they were alone.

"What do you mean?"

Alex sighed. "I'm worried that the killer might have seen her talking to you, too."

Annie studied his face. Alex was serious. He didn't look away from Annie's stare. He didn't fidget. Could she trust him?

"Why did she come here?" he asked again.

Annie shrugged and looked away. "I heard that the chef and Phil were at Bigger Burger together on Friday. I asked her if she remembered anything about them."

"Did she?"

"She remembered seeing you, Alex, and when she saw you here, she bolted." That wasn't exactly true but it was all Annie was willing to share for now.

Alex reached out and held Annie's arm. She flinched. He let go. "Sorry. I'm not the enemy. She served the chef a coffee before he left. A coffee that he left for Phil. Did she say anything about that?"

Annie nodded.

Alex crunched his mouth to one side and looked away. "I bet she saw something that I suspected. The chef dumped something in that coffee, didn't he?"

Jason clomped inside with the dogs. "All done with Leona's lesson?" He raised his eyebrows as he directed his question at Annie and moved next to her. He put his arm around her shoulders protectively. Annie shuffled closer to his side, relishing the safe embrace.

Alex continued. "I'll tell you what I think since that might be the only way you'll trust me. I've been doing some research, trying to fill in the gaps between what I know and what I suspect. What I've come up with is this: according to what the chef told me, he had a problem with someone; he and his assistant, which could be Phil, weren't getting along; Chef Marcel put something in Phil's coffee; Phil died after leaving Bigger Burger and before he arrived here for the workshop; the chef was murdered here before his workshop even started."

"You aren't telling me anything I didn't already know." Annie still refused to trust Alex.

"Right. Robin's comments got me thinking about something that the chef had access to. Something he might have used to poison Phil. What ingredient did the chef bring here for his pastry projects?"

"I haven't looked in his boxes, that's Leona's territory."

"Name one item you *know* he brought."

Annie put her finger on her chin and thought about what was in Leona's kitchen that Leona definitely didn't have before the weekend. Then, Robin's words made a new connection. "Leona chose her cherry buried cake recipe because she said the chef brought lots of cherries."

Alex smiled. "Exactly."

"Exactly what?" This conversation was going nowhere as far as she was concerned.

"You just heard what Robin said." Alex looked first at Annie, then at Jason. "If the pits are ground into a powder, it only takes a small amount to kill someone."

Both Annie and Jason stared at each other before looking back at Alex in disbelief. "The chef dumped ground cherry pits into Phil's coffee?" Annie asked.

"I *think* so but I don't have proof. Could you find out the cause of death from the police?"

"I doubt it. They might not even have that kind of information back from the lab yet."

"But Phil was poisoned, right?"

"According to the rumors . . . which have a way of being quite accurate at times."

"Okay. I think Tricia witnessed the chef putting some type of poison into Phil's coffee." Alex pulled his phone from his pocket. "Watch this." He tapped the screen and a video played of the chef standing at the counter with Tricia. She handed him a coffee and he turned away from Alex's view. His hand reached into his pants pocket and he pulled out a pill bottle but the rest wasn't visible to the camera. "Tricia was at a different angle and she saw what I couldn't see."

"*If* the chef killed Phil, Tricia shouldn't be in any danger since the chef is dead now too. But who killed *him*?"

Alex frowned. "I don't know. But I wouldn't jump to the conclusion that Tricia is safe."

A list of all the people, besides herself and Leona, that were at the Blackbird when the chef was murdered ran through Annie's brain—George, Sarah, Robin, Jared, Connie, Alex.

Who murdered the chef? And why?

The *why* of Chef Marcel's murder ate at Annie.

Was Alex really working for the chef?

Was Robin really writing a novel?

Did one of the others have a history with the chef who might like to see him dead?

As she stood in the entryway of the Blackbird with Jason and Alex, the unknowns of this murder gave her an uneasy pause. With the murderer still in her midst, everyone had to be extra vigilant.

23

J ason broke the silence. "Any chance that Leona has a fresh pot of coffee? I could use some to warm me up." He rubbed his hands together.

Annie jerked herself out of her own thoughts, blinked, and forced herself back to the present situation. "I'll make some. The cherry buried cake lesson should be wrapped up and Leona will want everyone out of the kitchen so she can get organized for dinner."

Jason turned to Alex and draped his arm over the man's shoulder as if they were best buddies. "That sounds good to me, how about you?"

Annie smiled at Jason's clever maneuver as he engaged Alex and moved him toward the living room.

"Ask Leona if she can spare a piece of cake, too," Jason said. "I promise it won't ruin my appetite for dinner."

After the late lunch they'd had at Bigger Burger, Annie knew Jason couldn't have much of an appetite but coffee and sweets was a great distraction. Alex had no choice but to stay with Jason while she got the coffee.

The kitchen was a disaster with chocolate ganache dripped on every surface, cherries squished on the floor, and pieces of chocolate cake lying next to every shape of finished project, but Leona had a smile from ear to ear. "Everyone loved the project. It was a bigger success than I could have imagined. They all want one more either tonight after dinner or tomorrow morning. What do you think?"

As Annie surveyed the mess, she was amazed that Leona wasn't tearing her hair out but, on the other hand, a mess indicated that people were busy. "How about tomorrow? This will take some time to get cleaned up and you have to get dinner for everyone. I think we should work on getting everyone fed and relaxed tonight so maybe we can uncover more information about each guest."

"That's a good idea. I'll get started with the grilled ham, cheese, and pineapple paninis for dinner if you can tackle the project disarray. Any suggestions for tomorrow's project?" Leona placed her big cast iron griddle across two stove burners.

"I'll think about it but first I have to make coffee and bring some cake out to the living room." Annie made quick work of measuring the coffee and water. As the rich, dark liquid dripped through the machine, she cut a few slices of cake. "I'll be right back."

The living room was cozy with Jason and Alex chatting near the fireplace; Connie, with Buddy on her lap, and Sarah sat together on the couch; George gazed at nothing from the chair in the corner; and Robin had her eyes glued to her phone, of course. Roxy was curled up on an empty chair and Annie spotted Trouble's tail twitching from under the same chair.

"Here's coffee and cake. Leona and I are getting dinner ready," she announced, even though no one seemed to pay her any attention. Good.

Back in the kitchen, Annie pulled a couple of cotton dish

towels from the drawer, got one wet, and carried them, along with a spray bottle, to the first work station. "Where do you want me to put these finished projects?"

"Just label them and that will be dessert tonight." Leona opened the fridge and started pulling her ingredients out.

Annie decided to tackle the messiest work place first. "There's no cake here, just a huge mess."

Leona chuckled. "Without turning around I can tell you're at Connie's spot. She kept nibbling on her cake until it was gone. I guess she thought if she took small enough bites, no one would notice that she ate the whole darn thing. I'll give her one of mine if she still has room for more."

"Connie? Room for dessert?" Annie felt her forehead wrinkle. "She loves her sweets. I don't think it's a question of having any room. If a delicious dessert is offered, she'll be the first to attack it whole heartedly."

The two women focused on their tasks at hand and made quick work of transforming the kitchen back to Leona's sparkling space.

"So," Annie said, interrupting the comfortable silence, "who do you think killed the chef?"

Leona paused, turned toward Annie, and leaned against the counter next to her big stove. "You know, I've been keeping my eye on Robin and I'd love to see all the videos on her phone. There could be a clue we've overlooked. And that George is a strange one. He seemed to have it in for the chef from the minute he got here. Has Alex discovered anything?"

"Hmmm. You're kind of hung up on Alex. I'm not ready to give him a pass yet. Especially not after Tricia, the waitress from Bigger Burger, freaked out when she saw him here."

"Oh?"

"Yeah. Alex was at Bigger Burger when the chef and Phil were having some sort of argument."

Leona flicked her wrist dismissively. "That doesn't prove anything, Annie. Alex told you that he's a private investigator working for the chef. Why would he kill him?"

Annie shrugged. "All I'm saying is he was here, he had the opportunity, and we don't know if everything he's told us is true."

The kitchen's back door opened and the sound of boots stomping on the mat made Annie and Leona look toward that entryway.

"Hello?" Leona called.

"Oh good, you're here. Is Annie here, too?" Camilla's voice filled the kitchen, along with the sound of her unzipping her coat, something heavy hitting the floor, mumbling, and finally more footsteps.

"I'm here, too. Come on in. We're just cleaning up and getting dinner ready for the guests."

Camilla walked in, a bright green silk scarf, which matched the streak in her hair, was wrapped around her neck. "I've come to apologize for rushing out the other night. I don't know what got into me but Tyler said nothing should change my relationship with you guys just because he and I are dating." She helped herself to a bite-size piece of cake at one of the work areas. "Yum." She licked her finger. "That was delicious."

"A leftover from Leona's workshop for the guests. With the chef dead and Tyler telling everyone to stick around town, it made sense to keep them busy baking rather than moping around like a bunch of kids waiting to be entertained."

"Yeah," Leona added. "The chef brought so many ingredients, it just made sense to set up some baking demonstrations for a distraction and to kill some time." She grimaced. "Hmmm, maybe not the best choice of words. Anyway, they all paid for the whole weekend, except Alex, but he has offered to reimburse me for the room. All in all, I think it's working out pretty well, right Annie?"

"Seems to be." Annie was suspicious that the distraction Leona referred to was more for her own benefit than her guests', but she could tell herself whatever she wanted. "How's everything in town, Camilla? I suppose the rumor mill is working overtime."

Camilla stuck out her bottom lip and blew a puff of air to get a few strands of hair out of her eyes. "That's an understatement. Everyone suddenly has a need to come into the Velvet Box thinking *I* know something. Apparently, along with the two murders, me dating Tyler is another big topic of conversation around town."

"Do they buy something or just get their fingerprints all over your glass cases?" Leona asked.

"Oh, sales are soaring. As a matter of fact, when three of your guests came in on Saturday morning, I had one of my best sales ever. That older woman must be loaded."

"Connie?" Annie asked. "Short gray hair, friendly, always talking?"

"That's the one. "She oohed and aahed over everything and bought one of my most expensive necklaces. The other woman bought some earrings after Connie hounded her to get *something* for herself even though she made it clear that she didn't want her husband to find out she'd spent any money."

Annie rolled her eyes. "That must have been Sarah. Her husband gave her this weekend at the Blackbird for a present but it wasn't what she wanted. Maybe that's why Connie convinced her to treat herself." Annie moved the empty plate to the sink and gave the counter one last swipe with her cleaning cloth. "What about the other person? Robin. She's a local and needed a ride back from the Black Cat Café after her boyfriend ditched her."

"Oh yeah. I thought I recognized her. She's been in with her mom a few times. She always wants to buy just one earring, which drives me mad, but I grin and humor her. What does she think I do with the other one?" Camilla shook her head. "Maybe

I'll set up a case for all the lonely single earrings," she said more to herself. "But I haven't told you the interesting part yet."

Camilla looked at Annie and Leona with a grin that indicated she'd just discovered a loose diamond in her pocket. A big one. "Well, Sarah spent a lot of time whispering to Connie about her husband."

Annie held her finger over her lips for Camilla to stop talking. She cracked open the door to the dining room and stuck her head out before she turned around to face Camilla. "Coast is clear, go ahead."

"Of course, I was right there showing Connie piece after piece of jewelry while Sarah got all her anxiety out. I was an invisible nobody to her while she griped. Finally, she admitted that she was worried about what was in her husband's suitcase."

Both Annie and Leona moved closer to Camilla. Camilla leaned on the kitchen island toward them with a glint in her eyes.

"What did Sarah say was inside?" Annie's heart raced, hoping this could be a clue to solving the chef's murder.

"Well," Camilla said slowly, obviously enjoying all the attention directed her way and wanting to drag out the best details the longest. She lowered her voice to barely above the faintest whisper. "Sarah thinks her husband could be the murderer."

Leona's eyes bugged out.

Annie gasped. "Did she say why?"

"After they went upstairs together before dinner on Friday night, what's his name?"

"George."

"Yeah, George was fuming about wanting a refund. Sarah got out the paperwork and showed him where it said no refunds, but he said he'd figure out something. Then he left their room but Sarah told Connie that she didn't know where he went or what he did. At the time, she was glad for a break from his endless ranting about Chef Marcel and how he suspected he was nothing more than a charlatan with a phony accent, a big belly, and a mustache." Camilla straightened. She adjusted the scarf, pulling it so it was looser on her neck. "She doesn't even want to stay in the same room with George anymore but she doesn't know what to do. Connie said she could share her room if it made her feel any safer."

"That *is* interesting. If George left their room, he could have slipped into the chef's room and confronted him about a refund. Maybe that's who Alex heard going into the chef's room Friday night," Annie said.

"There's more," Camilla continued. "George wouldn't let Sarah add anything to his suitcase. He packed his stuff and locked it, so she thinks he hid something inside that he didn't want her to find."

"If it had anything to do with the chef, Detective Crank must have found it when she intercepted George's attempt to skedaddle Friday night." Annie was thinking out loud. "This certainly puts a new light on Friday night's events." Annie turned back toward Camilla. "Did you tell Tyler all this?"

Camilla nodded. "Of course. It seemed important. And he didn't tell me to keep it secret," she quickly added. "Listen, I can't stay any longer. I'm meeting Tyler for dinner but I wanted to apologize and tell you all that stuff. I'll let myself out so you can get back to your dinner preparation."

"Thanks Camilla. Enjoy your date," Annie said.

"Oh, don't worry about that." She winked as she headed through the door to get her coat.

"No wonder George has been acting like a kid with his hand in the cookie jar. He must be hiding something," Annie said. "We'd better be extra careful around him."

"So, you're striking Alex off your suspect list?" Leona asked Annie.

"Not off completely, but I'll move his name to the bottom of the list for now."

Jason poked his head into the kitchen. "I could use some help out here . . . before there's another murder to report."

Annie and Leona dashed from the kitchen, following behind Jason.

Annie's head buzzed with concern—for what, she wasn't sure, but she knew Jason was a calm, cool, and collected person and would never pull the panic button for no reason.

24

A loud argument traveled from the living room into the dining room, but stopped suddenly when Jason entered in front of Annie and Leona.

George stood with his fists clenched, his face red, and his jaw clamped tight.

Sarah stood trembling about five feet away, her face drained of color as she stared at her husband. "All I asked is where did you go when you left our room Friday night? If you have nothing to hide, just tell us, otherwise . . ." Her voice trailed off to nothing.

"Otherwise, she's sleeping in *my* room tonight." Connie draped her arm over Sarah's and pulled her close.

All eyes focused on George.

He stomped from the room. Loud footsteps echoed up the stairs to the second floor. A door slammed, shaking the whole house.

Annie let her breath out. That problem took care of itself.

Sarah sniffled. "I can't believe this is happening. This weekend was supposed to be fun." She looked around the room. "What should I do now?"

"There, there," Connie crooned to Sarah. "Did you tell that detective about George leaving your room Friday night?"

Sarah's eyes bugged open wide. Her mouth opened and closed as she struggled to respond. Finally, in a small, little girl voice, she answered, "No. I couldn't say those words out loud and have the detective think George had the opportunity to kill the chef. It was just too much." She covered her face with her hands and sobbed.

"Maybe we should take a look in that suitcase of his," Annie suggested. "Maybe you'll find something that helps you understand his behavior." That was the gentle suggestion for what Annie was *really* thinking. She wanted to take a look to see if Detective Crank overlooked a clue. Sometimes you miss something that's staring you right in the face because you don't know *exactly* what you're looking for.

Before Sarah had time to pull herself together and respond to Annie's suggestion, a door opened above them. Everyone looked up. Footsteps echoed down the stairway and the front door opened and slammed closed with another house-rattling explosion.

"Okaaay." Alex wiped his hands together. "I think it's safe to say that George has decided he's had enough of all of us here at the Blackbird Bed and Breakfast."

"I wonder if he took his suitcase with him," Annie added.

Sarah's sobbing increased to a dramatic and pathetic nature. "I can't," she choked out between sobs, "believe . . . he left . . . without me."

"He's not supposed to leave town, so I wouldn't worry too much about him," Leona said. Her tone indicated *she'd* had about enough of the current drama. "He won't go far. Let him cool off before you go chasing after him."

Robin, who finally put her phone down, asked, "Are we getting any dinner around here?"

Leona rolled her eyes at Annie. "It's almost ready. Jason, could you pour drinks for whoever wants something while Annie and I finish up in the kitchen?" She muttered so only Annie could hear, "I thought the plan was to have a quiet and relaxing evening."

"Let's go upstairs and see if George left his suitcase in your room. That way you'll know if he's planning to return," Connie said to Sarah. "And don't you want to see what's inside?"

"I don't know." Sarah hesitated, her eyes terrified.

"I always say it's best to keep busy in times of stress." Without letting Sarah think about it too much, Connie looped her arm through Sarah's. "Come on, it will only take a minute to check."

"Annie?" She stopped at the sound of Robin's voice. "Jared wants to stop by, is that okay?"

"What for?"

"He said he has something to talk to me about and needs to do it in person. I told him I wasn't going anywhere and if he needed to talk to me he could come here."

"So, you asking me if it's all right is beside the point." Annie didn't know what to make of Robin and her attitude of entitlement. Was it her age or was she just a self-centered person?

"I guess it is." Robin smiled. "I'll check if he's here yet."

With only Jason in the living room with Annie and Alex at the moment, he pointed to the little table next to the chair where Robin usually parked herself. Her phone glowed from the flames from the fireplace. "Should we look at those videos she's always taking?" he asked.

Annie didn't bother to answer. She took five big steps to the table and snatched up the phone. It disappeared in her pocket. "Robin's distracted so maybe she won't miss it for a bit."

By the time Connie and Sarah returned with George's suitcase, Sarah was laughing. "I never thought of it that way," she said to Connie. "George would have had to go downstairs to get the leash off the coat tree before he went to the chef's room. That just doesn't make sense if he went to the chef's room to demand a refund. He wouldn't get a refund with the chef dead."

Whoever tightened that leash around the chef's neck was out to kill him. Annie suspected it didn't have anything to do with getting a refund from the chef. Did George have a different reason to want the chef dead?

"That's right. Now, do you have a key to open this suitcase?" Connie asked.

"I think so, but I'm still not sure I want to open it." Sarah sat on the couch with one hand on Buddy.

Annie quietly left the room as Jason filled four glasses with wine, hopeful that would keep Connie and Sarah occupied. Maybe she and Leona could finish the dinner preparation before a new interruption arrived. And, more importantly, to check what was on Robin's phone before she started looking for it.

No interruption turned out to be wishful thinking she soon discovered.

Detective Crank lounged against the island sipping on something in her travel mug. Leona had all the ingredients ready to start making her grilled paninis. Her big cast iron griddle was heating over two burners on her gas stove.

"So, I'm looking for Jared. Are you hiding him upstairs in the bathtub?" Christy asked with a straight face.

"That little weasel left on Saturday and I haven't seen him since," Leona said.

"Actually," Annie said, "Robin just informed me that he's supposed to be meeting her here. Go check at the front door to catch him before he comes and goes."

"Are you making any extras of those?" Christy was almost drooling as she eyed Leona's luscious panini creations on her way to the door.

"Unfortunately, these are all spoken for." Leona filled her grill with the paninis—including one with no ham for Jason. The sizzle made Annie's stomach rumble.

"That's a shame," Christy said as left the kitchen.

"What's she want with Jared?" Annie asked.

Leona turned the flame down. "She didn't tell me but I'm glad I'm not him. There isn't much chance that she showed up with *good* news."

"Check this out." Annie pulled Robin's phone out of her pocket. "Robin left it in the living room." She hit the home button and the screen came to life. "Great, it's not locked." She touched the photo icon. "It will take a while to watch all these videos. I'll start at the beginning, maybe something will look out of place now in hindsight."

While Leona tended to her grill, Annie watched Robin's videos. The first one was everyone sitting in the living room before Annie had even arrived. Chef Marcel complained about the weather and fidgeted with his mustache. Connie patted Buddy and asked the chef about his recipes. Nothing unusual.

The next video was in Robin's room after she'd taken food upstairs before dinner. This was more interesting because Jared was featured. He told her about his research into the chef's background and how he expected the chef would make a lot of money when his cookbook was released.

"Cookbook? The chef was working on a cookbook?" Leona asked.

Annie nodded. "There's more. Listen to this, Leona." Annie carried the phone closer to her aunt. Jared's face filled the screen as he said, "That guy must be loaded. I'm gonna check out his room while everyone is still downstairs." The video continued as Jared opened the door and walked out. The video followed him as he walked down the hall and opened the chef's door, disappearing inside.

Annie looked at Leona. "Jared went into the chef's room. But that was before the chef went upstairs so it must have been empty."

"Maybe Jared was still in the room when the chef got there. I was in the kitchen and you helped Connie upstairs after everyone else went up. And now Christy is here looking for Jared? Why did he come back here, anyway?"

"Robin told me that Jared needed to tell her something."

Leona turned the two burners off. "How long before Robin starts to look for her phone? Do you have time to look at any more of those videos?"

"I think I'd better put it back on the table. I'll figure out something to get her to let me look at them. I think she's a bit of a show off and if I flatter her she might share everything." Annie carried Leona's big salad bowl to the dining room table and continued into the living room.

With George's suitcase resting on the couch, still closed, Connie entertained Sarah with her baking disaster stories. Annie surreptitiously placed Robin's phone back where she'd found it. "So, you don't think the chef's cookbook will ever get published now?" she heard Sarah ask Connie.

That grabbed Annie's attention. Apparently, the chef's cookbook was common knowledge to the people who paid attention to him.

"I suppose it won't," Connie said. "I mean, how could it now with him dead? And I was looking forward to having a signed copy from him when it did come out. Wasn't that part of taking his workshop?"

Annie moved next to Jason, but continued listening to Connie and Sarah. Unfortunately, Sarah changed the subject and started to tell Connie about some recipe she had made recently.

"Did you see Christy walk through?" Annie asked Jason.

He nodded.

Annie lowered her voice. "She's here looking for Jared. I don't know what she's *after,* but one of Robin's phone videos made it clear that he went into the chef's room."

"Jared made a visit to the chef's room? Interesting," Alex said.

Annie moved closer to the door leading to the front entryway with the hope of hearing the discussion between Detective

Crank, Jared, and Robin. As those voices rose, everyone's attention was focused on the argument.

"Enough of your lies," Christy demanded. "I know you were in the chef's room."

"The chef wasn't in the room when I went in," Jared insisted.

"That might be true but I'll ask you one more time, Jared—did Chef Marcel come into his room while you were still there?" Annie could picture Christy with her arms crossed as she waited and her foot tapping as she stared at the quivering Jared. She almost felt sorry for him.

Silence as deep as a thick blanket of snow filled the Blackbird Bed and Breakfast. Everyone waited.

From around the corner of the living room doorway, Jared's shaky voice finally broke the hush with a soft whisper like the wind rustling a dry leaf. "He did come in but I had already hidden myself under the bed before he saw me."

Annie couldn't believe what she'd just heard.

25

C onnie gasped and her hand flew to her chest as if to calm a thumping heart.

Sarah's hand covered her mouth but not before a small eek slipped past her lips.

Annie looked at Jason, hoping he could read her what-does-this-mean expression.

Alex slipped Robin's phone into his pocket with only Annie noticing the quick move. He alone acted instead of being shocked into inaction by Jared's words.

Detective Crank entered the living room with Robin and Jared in tow. "Okay, folks, the show's over. Jared and Robin have agreed to come to the police station with me to answer the rest of my questions."

Robin glanced at the table where her phone should have been. She patted her pockets and glanced around the floor under the table. "Did anyone see my phone?" She directed her question toward Annie.

Annie shrugged, making a noncommittal answer that could mean anything.

"It must be in my room which is where I planned to leave it

anyway." Robin took another quick look around, patted the chair cushion, and sighed. "I'll find it when I get back. Can I get my dinner to go?" she asked, her voice noticeably absent of any concern about her upcoming trip to the police station. "I'd like to eat it while it's hot instead of coming back here, who knows when, to a cold, soggy meal."

"No problem." Annie headed toward the kitchen, glad to have something to occupy her body. "It will only take a minute to wrap it up for you." Was that *her* voice sounding so normal and unaffected by Jared's admission of being in the victim's room with him?

Annie pushed into the kitchen where Leona had all the dinner plates lined up on the island.

"Is everyone ready to eat?" She obviously had been busy with her meal preparation, and with her oldies station playing in the background she'd completely missed hearing any of the drama from the living room.

"Yes, but Robin needs her meal wrapped up to go and George is gone."

Leona turned from the stove with her spatula waving in front of her, punctuating each word as she spoke. "She's hiding out in her room again? Tell her she can eat at the table with the rest of us. If she keeps bringing food upstairs, I'll end up with more mice than guests!"

"Um, that's not exactly her situation. Robin and Jared are going to the police station with Christy."

"What?" Leona almost dropped the panini that was making the journey from the griddle to a plate when she jerked around to look at Annie.

"Yeah, Jared admitted to being in the chef's room. He said he hid under the bed before the chef came in, but I'm not sure Christy is buying that part of his answer." Annie wrapped one hot panini in foil, added a big slice of wrapped cherry buried cake, and a generous handful of cherries to a bag for Robin. Annie wouldn't put it past Robin to consider crushing the cherry pits to add to someone's coffee as a way to escape the police interrogation if Christy's questions became too rough. "I'll tell everyone to head to the dining room. I'm sure there will be plenty of chatter at the table tonight."

Christy pushed through the door into the kitchen. She eyed the plates, one empty, one sandwich still on the griddle, and one bag for Robin. "Is that sandwich on the griddle extra?" She tilted her head and raised her eyebrows giving a good impression of a begging puppy. "It's not like I'm asking for a handout but I certainly would remember this act of kindness if that last sandwich made it into a bag with my name on it."

Leona waved her hand. "Take it. I can always grill up more if George returns or if anyone wants seconds. But I'm not wrapping one up for Jared. He can go hungry, as far as I'm concerned, or Robin can share hers with him if she's so inclined. I don't like sneaky, wanting-everything-for-nothing, possible killers under my roof *or* expecting handouts."

Well that summed up Leona's feelings without mincing any words. Annie tore off another piece of foil. "Do you think Jared killed the chef?" she asked Christy while she made a big production of wrapping the sandwich for her. She tightly folded the long side over and made neat corner folds at each end.

Christy laughed. "What do you think, Ms. Hunter? As much as I'd love to share all the minute details of this case with you," her lip twitched at one corner, "I'd much rather hear what *your* gut feeling is telling you about this event."

Annie ignored the sarcastic tone of Christy's comment. "Actually, I don't think the time frame works for Jared to be the killer." She watched Christy's expression which remained stone-cold serious. "He went into the chef's room well before the chef was upstairs."

"And you know this how?"

"Ask Robin." Annie definitely wasn't going to mention the

video, which was currently in Alex's possession. That was Robin's deal.

"Oh, I will. Those two haven't told me everything they know yet." She took the two bags from Annie. "Thanks for the food. Did you add a slice of cake, too?" The tip of Christy's tongue moistened each corner of her mouth as if she was already tasting sweet morsels of chocolate ganache stuck to her lips.

Annie rolled her eyes but she sliced off another piece of cherry buried cake, wrapped it, and dropped it into Christy's bag. "Enjoy. Don't forget, you owe us one now."

"I'll be back to talk about that after I'm done with those two kids. They have no idea what kind of mess they've created for themselves."

"You think Robin is involved?"

"To the extent that she knows something. Don't worry, I'll get it out of her."

Annie grinned. "Oh, I'm not worried about that. You could get a macho teenager to admit to crying just by giving him your stink eye."

Christy frowned and her eyebrows scrunched together as she looked over the top of her dark rimmed glasses. "I'll let that slide." She tapped the bags of food. "Thanks."

Annie stepped in front of Christy and held her arm out to block the door. "Before you go, what about George? He moped around here like a hyena that snuck into the kitchen and swallowed all of Leona's food. He has to be guilty of something."

"Nothing I've been able to find yet but he's still on my radar." Christy pointed at Annie. "If you find something, let me know. And, *please*, don't try to do something heroic on your own."

"Of course not. Did Sarah tell you that George left their room when everyone was upstairs and before we discovered that the chef was murdered?" Annie hated to throw Sarah under the bus like that, but it was an important bit of information. By Christy's reaction, it was something she was not yet aware of.

Christy frowned. "I thought she was just a Nervous Nellie. It looks like I completely misjudged her, and that doesn't sit well with me. Don't let her know I'll be back to find out what else she's been hiding."

"Our focus," Annie included Leona with a wave of her hand, "is to get the Blackbird's name cleared and out of the news." By the time Christy returned, Annie might even have more information gleaned from Robin's phone and George's suitcase.

After Christy left with the bags of food, Annie juggled four plates. "You've got the rest?"

Leona nodded. "I'll be right behind you."

Jason was in the process of filling Connie's and Sarah's wine glasses. "Would you prefer a beer?" he asked Alex.

Alex grinned and nodded. "Yes, please. I think that would please my taste buds immensely."

"How about you two beautiful cooks?" Jason said, holding up the bottle of wine.

"You need to ask?" Leona responded. "Just fill 'em up, please." She set one plate in front of Sarah and the other in front of Connie whose wine glass was already half empty. "Grilled ham, cheese, and pineapple paninis. My bean salad is already on the table and I'll be right back with spicy crab-stuffed avocados."

"Oh, my," Connie groaned. "Do you share your recipes or are they top secret and you'd have to kill me if you told me?" She giggled. The wine must have already gone straight to her head.

No one else laughed.

Annie didn't miss Leona's flinch at Connie's request.

"Actually, I don't share my recipes. I'm in the beginning stages of planning a cookbook which will include all my baked goodies from the Black Cat Café and my Blackbird Bed and Breakfast meals so I'm keeping all my creations to myself for now. I'm sure you understand." Leona disappeared through the kitchen door.

"That's too bad. I suppose I understand but it's still a shame. Chef Marcel made it clear that he wouldn't share either and, now, well, all will be lost with his demise." Connie dabbed at the corner of her eye with an embroidered hankie. "I was so looking forward to having a copy of his book. Do you think someone else will finish it?"

"I assume it will be dealt with by his heirs," Annie said.

"I don't think he has any," Connie lamented. "All those recipes. Lost forever. Such a pity."

"I wouldn't jump to that conclusion just yet. If everything was well organized, I bet someone will take on the project of getting his hard work published."

After offering her crab-stuffed avocados to each guest, Leona sat at the head of the table, unfolded her napkin, and let it settle on her lap. "That would be a good question for Robin. She seems to know about the writing and publishing world."

"It could depend on how close Chef Marcel was to finishing and whether he kept good notes. You know how some cooks," Annie made a point to look at Leona, "don't actually follow a recipe because they have a sense for what needs to go together."

"That's not fair, Annie. I keep notes on all my creations, every single adjustment, tweak, and dash of flavor. Once it's perfected and taste-tested, I work up the final recipe. Actually, Robin gave me a great idea while we were making the cherry buried cakes earlier."

Everyone looked at Leona.

"Photos—mouthwatering photos of each step while creating a recipe. Beautiful photos catch people's attention and then they can't wait to give the recipe a try. I know I've been manipulated by eye appeal to try a recipe plenty of times."

Annie nodded her approval.

"And it's about time you dust off your camera and help me with this project," Leona said to Annie. "You've neglected your photographic talent for too long."

Before Annie could point out that running the Black Cat Café took up too much of her time at the expense of other interests, the front door opened.

Footsteps echoed on the hardwood floor as someone approached the dining room.

"Great. I haven't missed dinner," George said. He pulled out a chair and sat next to Sarah. "What? Don't stop talking on my account."

"Where have you been?" Sarah said, her voice filled with hurt.

"Nowhere, just walking around and thinking." He looked around the table, his gaze stopping on Leona. "I have a confession to make."

Sarah pushed her chair back as she stood. The force tipped it backward, sending it crashing to the floor. "You didn't do it, did you?"

George's face morphed from surprise to shock to anger. "What are you talking about, Sarah?"

26

"Is there any more of that wine?" George eyed the bottle next to Jason. "I could use a glass, please."

Jason passed him the bottle.

Everyone waited as he poured himself some wine, sipped it, and looked at everyone again. The silence was thick. Deep lines on George's face and dark circles under his eyes revealed how much of a toll stress and weariness were taking on him.

George set his glass on the table. "I've had time to do some thinking." He paused. "I have a problem. I think you've suspected as much, Sarah, and this weekend's events have made me face my demons."

"What have you done, George?" Sarah's voice whispered around the table like the flutter of a newly emerged butterfly. "Did you go into the chef's room?"

"The chef? This isn't about the chef. As much as I think he took all of us for a ride this weekend, I realize I have to let go of my anger and move on." George's dark eyes bore into Sarah. "Do you actually think *I* killed the chef?"

"What else could it be? You left our room. Where *did* you go?"

George tensed. His eyes blazed. "Is that what you *all* think?"

Annie couldn't hold her tongue for one second more while he dithered on with his long non-explanation. "Listen, George, you've been acting like a guilty criminal. If you didn't kill the chef, you'd better have a good explanation for where you went. An explanation that gives you an alibi when Detective Crank returns." She folded her arms and stared at George.

George's mouth fell open. "I can't believe it. I came back ready to unburden my guilt and all of you look at me like I'm a murderer. Just forget it. I'm getting my suitcase and finding another room where I don't have to endure these accusing stares." With both hands on the table, he pushed himself to a standing position. "Why don't you ask *Sarah* where she went that night? When I returned to our room, *she* was nowhere to be found."

Before George had time to leave the dining room, Alex blocked the doorway. "Not so fast. You aren't leaving until you show us what's in that suitcase."

"You're crazy." George shoved Alex but, with Alex being at least four inches taller and carrying a good twenty more pounds of muscle, the shove had no more impact than a toddler pushing a boulder.

"Sarah?" Alex's strong voice rang out but his eyes remained on George. "Did you leave your room like George stated?"

Sarah's face matched the ivory linen napkins. "Yes. I went looking for George."

"Liar!" George yelled. "We would have passed on the stairs when I came up."

"The front stairs?" Sarah asked, her voice gaining a bit of strength.

"Of course, the front stairs."

"I took the back stairs, hoping I'd find you looking for a snack in the kitchen but I never went all the way down when I heard talking. Oh dear, now I don't know what to think."

George laughed. "And here I thought you had snuck into the

chef's room and you thought I snuck into his room but we were both somewhere else. There is one more thing I haven't told anyone yet—when Sarah and I first went upstairs while the chef was still in the living room, someone must have slipped into his room and had just closed his door. If it hadn't been for the click, I might not have noticed. So, before you accuse *me* of anything *Alex*, was it *you* in the chef's room?"

"Actually, Jared already admitted to sneaking into the chef's room," Annie said. "You hearing the door click confirms he went in when the chef was still downstairs."

Both George and Alex relaxed their postures slightly. Alex moved to one side and held his hand out for George to go through the door first. "Your suitcase awaits. As long as nothing suspicious is inside, you can take it with you."

"*You* don't make the rules. Detective Crank already searched my suitcase and she didn't find anything." George shifted his eyes to Leona's buffet. Annie followed his eye movement and saw for the first time that something was different.

"Calm down, George," Annie demanded. "You planned to unburden yourself, so let's get back to that. I think I know what you're feeling guilty about so open your suitcase and let's get this over with." She walked past both Alex and George and led the way to the living room. His suitcase lay on the couch with Roxy curled up on one side, Buddy on the other, and Trouble on top.

Jason put a log on the fire, Alex blocked the door from the living room to the front entryway, and Sarah stood just inside, wringing her hands

Connie munched on her panini as if she was at a spectator event. "No sense letting all this deliciousness get cold." Crumbs fell from her mouth as her teeth crunched another bite from her sandwich.

Annie picked up Trouble and stroked the purring cat. "I'm sure Leona will be happy to reheat everyone's dinner when we're done in here."

George stuck a small key in the suitcase's lock. He unzipped the top but didn't lift it open. The muscles in his jaw worked overtime.

Annie reached around and with one strong movement, flipped the top up. Trouble leaped from her arms and disappeared under the couch.

The glint of something shiny caught Annie's eye. She reached under folded shirts and pulled out an object wrapped in tissue paper with one corner exposed. As she carefully unwrapped the tissue paper, a beautiful silver candleholder was revealed.

Leona gasped. "I welcomed you into my home and you stole from me?" If her piercing glare could kill, George would have been knocked to the floor in one second flat. He remained standing.

"Oh, George." Sarah's words dripped with pain. "You promised you would stop."

George dug around to the bottom of his suitcase and pulled out the twin candlestick holder. He handed it to Leona. "I'm sorry. Sarah's right, I did make a promise to her and that's why I came back. But when you all looked at me like I was some kind of murderer I lost my courage."

Annie touched George's arm. "You've done the right thing. No harm done, right Leona?"

Leona gave a slight nod as she clutched her treasures to her chest. "Didn't Detective Crank wonder about these when she searched your suitcase?"

George shrugged. "I told her I bought them as a surprise for Sarah. I've perfected my lying over the years to hide my compulsive stealing."

Sarah sobbed.

"I don't think this clears either of you, though," Annie said to George and Sarah. "You did leave your room. I'm sure Detective Crank will be grilling you both when she comes back."

"Don't forget," Connie piped up, "George admitted he went

downstairs, so he could have gotten Buddy's collar off the coat tree."

Sarah's mouth fell open. She moved close to George. "That's ridiculous."

"Is it?" One of Connie's eyebrows ticked up.

"Let's leave that to the detective. I'll reheat the paninis. You can all start on the crab-stuffed avocadoes if you like."

"And more wine?" Connie asked.

"I'll get the wine," Jason offered.

As they filed back into the dining room, Annie noticed that Connie moved her glass to the chair next to Alex instead of taking the spot where she had been sitting next to Sarah. Did she think he could protect her from the killer?

Annie followed Leona into the kitchen with a stack of cold paninis. "What do you think of what just happened out there?"

"My meal got cold and they won't taste as crispy and yummy now." She turned on the two burners under the cast iron griddle. "Oh, that's not what you meant, is it?"

"Not exactly. How are you feeling about George stealing from you?"

"Well," Leona turned around while she waited for the griddle to heat up, "I'll have to rethink how I decorate any area that's open to guests, that's for sure. It caught me completely by surprise and I can't believe I hadn't even noticed those candle-sticks were missing."

"Do you think his version of events clears him from being a suspect?"

"Not at all. He was out and about and so was Sarah. Their stories are convenient but I don't, for one minute, think that they would have confessed to murdering the chef."

"Yeah," Annie said as she got the dessert plates ready. "What we've got now is Jared, George, and Sarah all wandering around when the chef was in his room. Any one of them could have done something while they were out."

Leona slid each sandwich onto the hot sizzling griddle. "What about Robin, Alex, and Connie?"

"Alex said he heard the chef's door open and close several times so who knows which one of them might have slipped into his room."

"Of course, Alex is in the room next to the chef."

"Right, and I helped Connie to her bed and she was snoring when I left. Robin? Who knows what she was up to? She could have followed Jared into the chef's room and stayed."

Jason pushed the door open into the kitchen. "Can you make a few extra paninis? This is a hungry group out here. Maybe bring in the first batch before you start on the extras."

"Sure. These are ready if you want to bring them to the table." Leona stacked the reheated paninis on a platter and handed it to Jason. She placed one to the side. "That one is for you without any ham."

"No problems out there?" Annie asked.

"Not as long as you don't run out of wine." Jason winked at her before he disappeared behind the swinging door.

"I'll need more pineapple. Can you look over there?" Leona pointed to a stack of crates in the corner. "That's all the ingredients that Chef Marcel brought. I'm trying to use his food before I dig into what I bought."

Annie lifted the top crate, filled with spices, nuts, and melting chocolate, off the pile. The crate underneath had oranges, apples, cherries, and a pineapple. The aroma of fresh fruit drifted to her nose as she lifted out the pineapple. "Chef Marcel brought more food than this crowd would be able to eat. Did he give you any idea of his plans for all this stuff?"

Leona joined Annie. She wiped her hands on her apron. "Unfortunately, he didn't. He stacked it all here and told me not to touch anything. He probably didn't want to share any of his secrets with me." She reached into a third crate. "I haven't even gone through everything yet. This one is full of different types of flours and sugars. Agave nectar? I wonder what he was going to use this for."

As Leona lifted out the container of agave nectar, an envelope was stuck to the bottom. "Huh, what's this?" She held the nectar container between her arm and side as she opened the envelope. "Well, well, well."

"What?" Annie straightened and peered over Leona's shoulder.

"It looks like his recipe plans for the weekend. I bet Connie would love to see this."

"Don't show her. Isn't that evidence?" Annie said.

"Evidence? Of what?"

Annie shrugged. "I don't know.

Leona shuffled through the index cards. "We can look, though, don't you think?"

"And take a lesson from Robin." Annie slid her phone from her jeans pocket. She clicked photos of each card. "Okay, got them. Put it back."

Leona slid the cards back into the envelope but they didn't want to go in. "There's something else in here." She pulled out a crumpled piece of paper.

Annie snatched it from Leona's hand and smoothed it flat. After she read the note, she looked at Leona. "Alex said that Chef Marcel had a problem with someone. Maybe this threatening letter is what he was referring to."

"What does it say?" Leona tried to take the paper but Annie turned away from her.

"*Bring the draft of your cookbook for me or I'm going public with your scam,*" Annie read out loud. "And it's signed with a *P*."

Annie and Leona stared at each other.

"Phil? Scam?" they both said at the same time.

"Is *this* why Phil was killed? He threatened to expose a scam?" Leona asked, her arms clutching Annie's shoulders.

Annie turned and crashed smack into Alex. "You found something?" he asked. His eyes searched her face.

Before Annie could answer, Leona blurted out, "You won't believe what we found."

Alex's eyes narrowed.

The hairs on Annie's neck rose.

Screeching filled the kitchen.

"Oh no!" Leona dashed to her stove. "My paninis are burning up."

27

J ason, followed by the remaining guests in the dining room, pushed through the kitchen door. He quickly shut off the two gas burners. "What's going on in here? Haven't you had enough drama with the power outage and a murder?"

Annie could see the concern etched on Jason's face. She felt bad that she'd left him at the dining room table for so long while she and Leona dawdled in the kitchen.

Connie leaned against the island, supporting herself, instead of crashing to the floor.

Roxy and Buddy barked and ran circles around the kitchen until the smoke alarm was silenced.

"Sorry. Everything's under control." Annie made a waving gesture with her hands, trying to shoo everyone out of the kitchen so they could clean up the burned-to-a-crisp mess. "We got distracted after Leona started to make more paninis and we had to look for one more ingredient. Just an oversight on the hot griddle. No problem."

George frowned. "Maybe you need more cooking lessons before you burn this place down. Or maybe that's your intent," he said with disgust in his voice. "You can't keep the lights on during a storm, a guest is murdered, and now," he waved his arm around the smoky kitchen, "you try to burn this place down. Are you so desperate for the insurance money that you put all of our lives in danger?"

Leona's jaw dropped at the insult. Annie pushed her toward the stove and away from George. "Jason, would you mind escorting our guests back to the table, please?"

Jason raised one eyebrow, gave Annie a slight nod, and held his arms out in an attempt to herd George, Sarah, and Connie out of the kitchen.

Connie fanned the smoke away from her face. "I'm all set with the panini I already enjoyed." She glanced at the blackened bread in a pile next to the stove. "Could we move on to dessert? There is dessert, I hope."

"Great idea," Annie gushed. "Dessert will be out in a jiffy."

George pulled Sarah's arm and followed Connie out.

Jason lingered at the door. "What's really going on?" he asked Annie. "Something distracted you to take your attention away from the stove?"

Annie pulled the paper from Leona's grasp. "We found this along with the chef's recipes for the weekend."

Now it was Alex's turn to raise an eyebrow in surprise. "His recipe plans for the weekend?"

"And this." Annie shoved the paper under Jason's eyes. "Read it."

It only took Jason seconds to scan the paper. Twice. He handed it to Alex. "You better show this to Detective Crank, Annie. It certainly gives Chef Marcel a motive to kill Phil."

"But who killed the chef?" Annie asked. "Do you think his killer stole the manuscript from his room?"

"Hold on a second," Alex interrupted. "You're jumping to conclusions here. There is more than one possibility."

Leona, Annie, and Jason looked at Alex.

"First," Alex raised his index finger, "maybe the chef didn't even bring his manuscript. Second," his middle finger joined his index finger, "maybe the chef did give the manuscript to Phil and the police have it. Or third, the chef didn't give his manuscript to Phil but brought it here to the Blackbird and someone stole it like you suggested, Annie."

"You could have stolen it," Annie said. "You were upstairs while most of us were still down here in the living room before dinner. You could have slipped into the chef's room and stolen the manuscript."

"Why?" Alex asked with a tinge of anger in his voice. "What do *I* want with a rough draft of a cookbook?" He took a deep breath and continued, "This is the way I see it—figure out the scam that Phil mentioned, and that will lead us to his murderer; figure out who stole the manuscript to lead us to the chef's killer."

"So you suspect two killers?"

Alex nodded.

Annie deflated a bit. Alex had good points. Was it time to stop thinking about him as a suspect and start cooperating with him instead?

As if Alex could read her mind, he pulled Robin's phone from his pocket and handed it to Annie. "Here. You should take charge of this. If there's anything important, it's on you to decide what to do with the information."

Annie nodded her appreciation. She had forgotten about Alex having Robin's phone and this simple gesture helped her make up her mind about him.

Leona stood off to one side shuffling through the recipe cards. She picked up the handwritten note found with them. Her eyes moved back and forth between the different documents. "Take a look at this and tell me what you guys think." She handed everything to Annie.

Annie read the recipe cards and the note. She shrugged and was about to hand everything to Jason but jerked her hand back and held one of the recipe cards next to the note. Her heart pounded. "This is significant. It's all the same handwriting."

Jason and Alex leaned over her shoulder, took several seconds to study the writing, and nodded their agreement.

Leona said, "Either Chef Marcel wrote the note to himself for some crazy reason—"

"Or he was using Phil's recipes," Annie finished Leona's sentence. "Wow. Is that the scam? Phil was the mastermind behind the cookbook and he demanded his cut from Chef Marcel?"

Annie pushed through the kitchen door into the dining room on a mission. She barely noticed what Connie's chatter to George and Sarah was all about but she was glad the three weren't just sitting in silence.

"Is dessert on the way?" Connie asked.

"Just about. Have another glass of wine while you wait, "Annie said as she breezed through to the living room. She searched through a pile of papers on one of the tables and found what she was looking for.

Back in the kitchen, she opened the workshop brochure to the section where the chef had written a note to Connie. Annie pointed to the words on the brochure and read them out loud, *"Good luck with your éclairs. -Chef Marcel."*

"That writing doesn't match with the others," Leona stated the obvious. "See how the chef's letters on this brochure are printed in all caps. All his letters are vertical and written with a heavy hand. The recipes are written in a neat flowing cursive style. They couldn't be any more different from each other."

Annie summed up her thoughts. "I think the chef conned Phil into giving him recipes for this weekend's workshop, stuffed them in the envelope with the demand letter, added something to the coffee that killed him, then hoped to figure out a way to cancel the workshop. The snowstorm and power outage were the perfect excuses for him . . . if he hadn't gotten murdered."

"That's all well and good," Jason said, "but who killed the chef?"

Annie's mouth puckered in frustration. "We're right back where we started. Jason, go check on the guests and tell Connie dessert is on the way."

He nodded and left.

Alex fidgeted. "Can I help with something?"

Annie made a quick decision and this time she was one hundred percent sure when she decided to put her trust with Alex. "Yes, go up to Robin's room and take a look around before she gets back. Don't move anything, just look."

"Are you sure?" Leona asked. "If he gets caught in a guest's room, it won't look good for my reputation."

"Good point. I'll do it." Annie handed Alex the dessert plates and forks. "Alex can help you serve dessert."

Leona's face relaxed. "Get a stack of fresh towels from the upstairs linen closet just in case Robin returns. It won't look so suspicious if you're in her room exchanging her towels."

"What are you looking for, Annie?" Alex asked as he paused at the door leading into the dining room.

"I don't know, but she's not here and it will satisfy my curiosity to take a quick look around." Annie waved the phone in front of Alex. "I need to put this in her room, too." She turned her attention to her aunt. "Don't worry, Leona, Robin will never know I was in there."

As Alex pushed through the door with the dessert plates, contented sounds of conversation floated into the kitchen. "Yes, here comes dessert," Connie screeched.

"Well, I've got the plates and forks but I'll be right back with dessert," Alex replied.

Good, Annie thought. Everyone would be occupied and as long as Robin didn't return in the next ten or fifteen minutes, she'd have time to see if there was anything that Detective Crank missed when she searched all the upstairs rooms after the chef was murdered.

Annie climbed the back stairs, two at a time, and grabbed a stack of towels from the linen closet. Leona had them color coded by room but Annie didn't bother to try to remember if Robin had the blue towels or the green ones. It would all get sorted out in the wash. She chuckled at her own silly joke which helped ease the nervous tension for her task.

The door into Robin's room was locked but Annie had a master key and made quick work of unlocking the door and slipping inside. She flipped on the light and was pleased to see that the shades were down which might help hide the fact that she was inside if Robin returned from the police station soon. She gathered up the dirty towels and hung fresh ones as she examined the room.

The bed was neatly made, a pair of slippers waited on the small rug next to the bed, and the antique desk had a stack of papers under a notebook with several black pens carefully lined up on top. No computer was in sight. Robin was neat and tidy and well organized, Annie observed. Robin's small suitcase was closed and sitting on top of a chair. Annie paused as she considered whether she dared to open it. She decided not to.

She tossed Robin's phone on the bed thinking that looked like an obvious place where she might have forgotten it.

As Annie stood in the center of the room with everything seeming to be exactly where it should be, Robin's words from Saturday surfaced from her memory. Hadn't Robin said she knew who killed the chef? It could have just been a boastful statement to shock Annie, or maybe she *did* know something.

Annie's focus returned to the desk. Robin mentioned that she spent time writing down her ideas when she went to her room. She could peek at the notebook. Annie took a step toward the desk, and then another. She hesitated. Before she could stop her hands they picked up the notebook, sending the pens rolling to the floor.

"What do you think you're doing?" Robin's voice sent a jolt of panic straight to Annie's heart. She must have come straight upstairs when she returned without anyone seeing her.

How did Annie not hear Robin approaching? Was she so lost in her own thoughts that she didn't hear the muffled footsteps? "I brought you clean towels and, you know, I'm such a klutz sometimes. I bumped into the desk, the pens rolled off, and I caught your notebook before it slid off, too." Annie's excuse came out easily and it even sounded reasonable to her own ears.

"Yeah, well, you can leave now." Robin snatched the notebook from Annie's hand. When she bent down to scoop up the pens, Annie glanced at the papers that had been hidden by the notebook. Recipes? She reached for the papers. Robin's hand caught Annie by the wrist. "What do you think you're doing?"

Annie shook Robin's hand off and glared at the younger woman. "*You* have Chef Marcel's manuscript?"

"It's not what you think," Robin said, her voice coming out barely above a whisper.

28

Annie crossed her arms and spoke through gritted teeth. "What *do* I think, Robin? Reading minds is a talent of yours?"

A smug grin spread across Robin's face. "You think I killed the chef and stole his manuscript. At least, that's what the obvious clues would suggest . . . but that's not what happened." She smirked.

"Okay. Tell me your version." Annie wasn't buying any of Robin's theories. For now. She was too smug, too cavalier, and much too cocky for her own good.

Robin crossed her arms to match Annie's stance and stared right back at her. "Maybe the chef gave me his manuscript . . . for safe keeping . . . because he identified with me as a fellow writer and," she paused for dramatic effect, "he suspected that someone wanted to steal it."

Annie choked on a laugh. "Maybe, but you're giving yourself an awful lot of credit with that line." She picked up the manuscript. "I agree with you that someone killed the chef over this pile of papers, but do I think that's you? I'm not sure. But since Jared already confessed to being in the chef's room, I would put him above you as the top suspect. By the way, how was your visit to the police station with Detective Crank?" Annie felt a tremor run through her body just from the thought of sitting in a small room with the detective.

"Piece of cake. She thinks she's all toughness and intimidation, especially after she separated us to ask her questions. I suppose she expected me to fall apart into a quivering mass of Jell-O but I gave her what she wanted and she let her guard down. I'd even go as far as to say she turned on her charm to make me think we were some kind of buddies."

"Charm?" Annie almost choked. "I'd never put charm and Detective Crank in the same sentence. What exactly did you tell her?" Robin's confidence level only seemed to have risen after her time with Christy.

"The truth. I have nothing to hide. I gave her my timeline of Jared's movements and told her what he told me, including how he peed himself when he was hiding under the chef's bed."

"You're kidding! How could you embarrass him like that? He's your friend."

Robin shrugged. "I think she might have already figured it out. Have you checked under the bed for urine? Besides, I wanted the detective to have some sympathy for Jared. Don't you think that if someone is so scared they pee themselves, they probably aren't brave enough to be a killer? I think it shows Jared to be exactly who he is—a big wuss."

Annie had to admit that Robin had a good point. Sort of. She'd found him quaking in the bathtub in Robin's room right after she and Leona discovered the chef's body. He certainly didn't look or act like a murderer then. "That's all interesting but it doesn't explain how this," Annie slapped the thick manuscript on the desk, "ended up here."

"Jared stole it," Robin said with a quick shrug of her shoulders. "He said it was under the chef's bed when he was hiding there. He assumed it had to be worth *something*."

"Let me get this straight. Jared went into the chef's room, heard him coming, hid under the bed, peed himself, but still focused enough to steal the chef's manuscript."

"I never said he was particularly smart. Jared told me he was bored and was going to poke around, see if he could find anything interesting. He *never* expected to be a witness to a murder." Robin picked up the manuscript and tapped all the pages on the desk to line them up before she set it back down in the exact middle of the desk.

Annie pulled on Robin's arm, forcing her to turn around and face her. "He witnessed the murder and it has taken the two of you this long to come forward with this information? After two people are dead? What were you waiting for, a third body to turn up in a closet or something like that?"

Robin moved her suitcase to the floor and relaxed into the chair with her legs crossed. "My choice of words wasn't the best. Jared didn't exactly *witness* the murder since he was under the bed and the dust ruffle hid him from being seen or from him actually seeing anything. But he was in the room when he heard someone come in, the chef gasped, then made a gurgling choking noise before it all went quiet. It's not too much of a leap to assume it was the murderer in the room. Jared also heard that person shuffling around like they were looking for something, or at least that was Jared's conclusion based on the noises he heard. Once he heard the door open and close again he rolled out from under the bed and saw the chef with his tongue out and eyes bulging. He had to clamp his hand over his mouth to stifle a scream before he managed to make it back to my room. Honestly, I never saw anyone with less color in their face."

"Who, Jared or Chef Marcel?"

Robin chuckled. "Nice try with that subtle trap, but I never saw the chef when he was dead."

"So, what are you going to do with the chef's manuscript?" Annie asked.

"I haven't decided yet. I'm not even sure if the detective knows about it. If I tell her that Jared stole the manuscript, she will see it as a motive for him and I don't want to give her any more ammunition against him. Once I figure out who *did* kill the chef, that's when I'll turn it over."

"I recall that you already told me you knew who killed him."

"I lied." Robin stood without showing any embarrassment about that particular behavior. She picked her phone up off the bed and slipped it into her pocket. "Time for you to leave. You've already wasted too much of my time."

If Robin so easily admitted to that one lie, what else was she lying about? Annie thought it was a well thought-out story that Robin presented to her but was it truth or part of Robin's fictional imagination? As soon as she was allowed back in the chef's room, she planned to check under the bed for that bit of evidence from Jared but she certainly wouldn't tell Leona what might be there on the floor. Not yet, at least.

Annie returned to the dining room and slid onto the chair next to Jason. He gave her one of his where-have-you-been looks but she just patted his thigh. This wasn't the time or place to share what she'd learned from Robin. "Any cake left?"

"Oh, Annie, Leona's cherry buried cake is to *die* for." Connie's voice rose an octave on the word 'die.' "To die from eating too much chocolate couldn't be such a bad way to go, right?" She didn't wait for a response but looked at the tray which only had a few cake crumbs left on it. "I'd love another piece so Annie doesn't have to eat all by herself."

Leona rolled her eyes as she stood. "I'll bring in more dessert. And coffee?"

"Oh, yes, you read my mind," Connie giggled. "I need something to wake up my brain after all that wine I drank."

Alex followed Leona into the kitchen, leaving Annie and Jason to carry the conversation with the guests.

"Robin is back from the police station," Annie said. She carefully watched everyone's reactions.

Connie's eyebrows rose.

George frowned.

Sarah twisted her napkin into a tight wad.

"What about Jared?" Connie asked. "They both left together."

"He's not here but I didn't ask if he's still being questioned. He was in the chef's room, after all, so he's in a tough spot and it wouldn't be surprising if it takes longer for the detective to question him."

George threw his napkin on the table. "I wish that detective would figure all this out so we could leave. One more day is all I intend to hang around. We did pay for tonight, anyway."

"Leona is planning another cooking session in the morning, dear. Aren't we going to stay for that?" Sarah said as she looked at her husband hopefully.

"Of course. We have to get our money's worth somehow. Not that it's a fair deal in my opinion. We paid for Chef Marcel's expertise, not some part-time cook who almost burned the place down."

Annie felt her eyes pop open with that comment and was glad Leona wasn't back in the room yet.

Alex entered with the coffee pot, followed by Leona with a tray of cake slices. Her face sagged with weariness but she managed a smile as she placed the tray on the table. "Don't worry George, next time I'll be sure to start the fire in the room that you're staying in so you have something to *really* complain about."

Annie faked a cough to cover her laugh. Apparently, there was nothing wrong with Leona's hearing. She filed that away for the future.

George's face turned beet red. He pushed his chair back from the table, stood, and stomped from the room.

"He needs to learn to keep his comments to himself," Leona

said more to herself than to the others who all looked at her, some with stunned expressions and some with amusement.

Alex laughed. "Serves him right. All he has done this whole weekend is gripe and complain as if it was *your* fault for what happened, Leona. Don't let him get under your skin."

"That's right," Connie agreed. "Your cooking is amazing, and so what if you burned that batch of paninis. Everything else was perfect."

Leona pinched her lips together but managed to refrain from giving Connie a piece of her mind, too. A compliment wrapped inside an insult wasn't worth much.

Robin poked her head into the dining room. "Oh good. I thought I smelled coffee. And more dessert, too? Great. I wouldn't mind another piece."

"Here, Robin," Connie stood, "take my seat. I'm tired after all the excitement from today. I'll take my coffee upstairs." She filled her mug and helped herself to another slice of cake. "I don't want it to go to waste," she said with a sheepish look on her face.

Sarah followed Connie out, wringing her hands as usual.

"Well, do I have bad breath or something?" Robin asked. "I never managed to send people from a room so quickly in my life. She sat in the chair where Connie had been and chose the biggest slice of cake.

"How is Jared holding up?" Alex asked. "Is he still at the police station?"

"Yup." She wrapped her mouth around a huge portion of cake balanced on her fork. After she swallowed, her tongue cleaned up a few crumbs at the corner of her lips. "Delicious. You know, that detective ate her panini in the car while she was driving. What a mess she made but she licked every bit of grease off her fingers."

That didn't surprise Annie. She knew Christy loved everything Leona made. "How did you get back here?" Annie asked. It had just occurred to her that Christy drove Robin and Jared to the police station.

"Some cop gave me a ride. Detective Crank was still busy with Jared. My guess is that she might be coming back here when she's done with him. She asked me a lot of questions about George and Sarah but I couldn't tell her much about them. I'm pretty sure she'll show up at some point to grill them some more."

Robin used her finger to get the last of the crumbs off her plate. "Speak of the devil," she said with a nod toward the dining room door. "Company has arrived." Robin leaned back in her chair and looked like she was comfortably settling in to enjoy some type of show.

Detective Crank walked to the table. Her normally tight ponytail was a bit looser than normal with several hairs floating free. A few grease splatters speckled her wrinkled shirt. She sighed. "I was planning to go home and get some rest but I changed my mind since I have a few questions that keep swirling around. Could you ask George and Sarah to come down and find the three of us a private spot to talk?"

Annie poured Christy coffee without asking if she wanted any and handed her a plate with cake at the same time. "Sit down for a minute while I run upstairs and find them."

"Thanks. This will give me an energy boost to get through the rest of the evening."

When Annie knocked on George and Sarah's door, she heard a grumpy response. "Who's there?"

"It's Annie. Could you two come downstairs please? Detective Crank has some questions."

The door flew open. "What does she want *now*?" George glared at Annie.

"I don't know, but the sooner you come down the sooner it will be over." Her patience with this bore was razor thin.

"She wants me, too?" Sarah asked, her voice betraying a definite nervousness.

"Uh-huh. Both of you."

The door slammed closed in Annie's face. "If you don't come down in five minutes I'll send her up here." Annie wanted to go home, too, but she wasn't planning to abandon Leona with this drama unfolding.

George stomped from his room.

Sarah followed close behind.

Annie shook her head wondering when and, more importantly how, it would all end.

29

Annie paused outside George and Sarah's room after they went downstairs. She stared at the doorknob. Her hand twitched. Did she dare sneak a peek inside?

"Annie?"

She squeaked in surprise at hearing her voice. Her hand, which had been slowly moving toward the doorknob, flew to her chest instead. Getting caught even *thinking* about doing something unethical was a shock to her system.

"Connie? You startled me."

"I *see* that." Her voice hinted at suspicion. "Are George and Sarah in their room?"

"Not at the moment." Annie moved away from the door. "Everyone is downstairs I think."

"Oh. I have a favor to ask. Buddy could use a bit of fresh air and I'm in the middle of organizing my things." She sighed. "As much as I've enjoyed this weekend, I have to leave tomorrow along with the other guests and I've made such a mess of my room. I don't want to leave it all to tomorrow." She held out Buddy's leash. "Would you mind?"

Annie looked at the dachshund. "Of course, I don't mind."
She'd do it for Buddy. "A bit of fresh air will do me good, too."

"Don't hurry, I've got a lot to organize between Buddy's paraphernalia and all of my belongings. I always bring too much stuff
when I go somewhere." She closed her door, leaving Annie alone
with the dog.

Annie slipped the leash into her pocket and led the way to the
stairs. "That was a close call for me, Buddy. Good thing Connie
can't read minds."

Roxy sat in front of the door, thumping her tail on the floor.
"You heard Buddy's nails on the stairs and figured out what we're
doing?" Annie opened the door and the dogs dashed outside.
Stars twinkled overhead and the smell of wood smoke wafted to
Annie's nose. She breathed in deeply, cleansing her lungs with
the cold winter air as she watched the two dogs sniff and pee and
sniff some more.

"Hey, want some company?" Jason's voice drifted from the
darkness.

Annie smiled. "Leona has everything under control inside?"

"I hope so. She closed the living room door with Detective
Crank, George, and Sarah inside. Robin is sitting at the dining
room table while she inhales coffee, and Alex is helping Leona in
the kitchen. I felt like I had nowhere to go so when I heard the
front door open and close, I came out to investigate." Jason put
his arm around Annie's shoulders. "I'm glad I did."

Annie leaned into the snug curve he created for her. She
stuck her hands into her pockets. A chill ran down her spine. "I
need to go inside and check something. Will you keep an eye on
the dogs?"

"Abandoning me already?" Jason teased.

"Just for a minute." She kept her voice steady.

"Okay then, but I'll hold you to it."

Annie went inside. The living room door was still closed.
Except for a few sounds coming from the kitchen, all was quiet.

She took the stairs two at a time, hoping her gut instinct was wrong.

With the carpet muffling her footsteps, Annie walked to Connie's door. She turned the knob without a knock.

Connie turned, blinking quickly several times. "Back already? I thought Buddy would want to spend more time outside." Her eyes traveled from Annie's face to the space around her. "Where's Buddy? Did you lose him?" Panic filled her voice.

"No. Jason is outside with Buddy."

Connie's hand moved to her forehead. "Oh, thank goodness. You really gave me a fright." She flipped the top closed on a suitcase on her bed. "Well, that one is all set." She pointed to another suitcase on the floor. "Could you lift that up here next to this other suitcase? It's a bit too heavy for me."

Annie quickly looked around the room. What was she doing in here? What made her feel like icy fingers were suddenly around her neck? She lifted the suitcase. For its size, it was surprisingly heavy. "What's in here, rocks?"

Connie giggled. "Lots of papers. I never mentioned this to anyone here, but I fancy myself as a bit of a writer. Unfortunately, my stories never go anywhere, but I do research and keep plugging away."

Annie plopped the suitcase on the bed but she misjudged the distance from the other one. One corner caught on the first suitcase, knocking the other off balance and sending it toward the edge of the bed. The movement jiggled the top open just as it tipped over the edge of the bed.

Connie was not exaggerating when she said the suitcase was full of papers. But what a bizarre collection spread across the floor in front of Annie—pictures of Chef Marcel, newspaper articles about Chef Marcel, and Chef Marcel's brochures. The last pile of papers to land at Annie's feet was the manuscript she had seen in Robin's possession.

"What is all this?" Her brain wasn't quick enough to catch up with what her eyes were looking at.

"Oh dear," Connie said before Annie felt hands on her back, shoving her to the floor.

Even though Annie was stronger and taller than Connie, the surprise shove from behind caught her off guard. As she crashed to the floor, she reached into her pocket for the leash—Buddy's *blue* leash which had no business being in Connie's possession. The only explanation that flashed through Annie's brain in that fraction of a second was that Connie had *two* blue leashes. One that she used to strangle Chef Marcel and was now evidence in Detective Crank's possession, and this other one that she kept as a secret decoy until she could remove it from the coat tree and hide it. Clever. Except for the fact that she forgot her own scheme.

Connie lunged toward Annie but slipped on all the papers, falling and crashing on top of her. She yanked Annie's hair and tried her best to keep the upper hand.

Annie managed to fling the leash around Connie's arm, catch both ends, and yank it to one side, pulling Connie off. In one nimble movement, Annie was on top of Connie with her arms pinned to the floor. Under Connie's head was brochure after brochure of Chef Marcel's smiling face with words encouraging her to keep baking.

"Didn't the chef put two and two together when you signed up for this workshop?" Annie asked. "All this makes me think you've been stalking him for years."

"The pig didn't even offer a smile when I first saw him here." Connie's eyes had turned dark and narrow. "*Look* at all the signed photos he sent to me. He even signed them *love, Chef Marcel*. He led me on; made me think we could be partners. I thought we had a cosmic connection, something special, but he laughed at me when I told him face to face. He laughed. The man I devoted these last three years to. I couldn't believe it. What else could I do to save face?"

"What else? How about walk away from an egotistical narcissist?"

"Oh no, he got exactly what he deserved. He killed Phil, didn't he? His partner. I thought that was all part of his plan to make room for me." Spittle dribbled out the sides of Connie's mouth as she railed against Chef Marcel. Her head flailed back and forth. Her eyes focused on nothing.

Annie used all her strength to keep Connie pinned to the floor. The woman was stronger than she looked.

Just as Annie felt Connie give one extra big buck underneath her and she started to slip, she heard toenails clicking on the wood floor. Buddy and Roxy tore into the room. "We heard a crash," Leona said from right behind the two dogs.

"Are you okay?" Jason rushed to Annie's side, kneeling next to her.

Annie felt Connie's body lose its strength.

Detective Crank stood behind Leona. With Jason's help, Annie slowly rose and stood to one side of Connie. The leash dangled from her hand. "Another blue leash. What a clever diversion."

Connie sputtered that Annie had tackled her and why wasn't someone arresting *her*.

Robin stood in the doorway with her phone raised as she scanned Connie's room for her latest video. "My trap worked," she said with a grin on her face.

"Trap?" Annie asked. "What are you talking about?"

Robin pointed. "The manuscript. When you said someone killed the chef for the manuscript, I made sure to leave it in plain sight with my door unlocked. I suspected that whoever was willing to kill for it wouldn't stop searching until they found it."

"Thanks for the heads up." Annie scowled. "Your stunt could have gotten me killed, too."

"But it didn't." Robin picked up the manuscript. "I knew Jared wasn't the killer, or me, which narrowed it down to George,

Sarah, Alex, and Connie. I have to admit that Connie was at the bottom of the list." She flipped through the manuscript pages. "This is mostly a bunch of blank pages anyway. The only thing Chef Marcel was an expert at was fooling people. I don't think that he actually knew how to make the perfect éclair or any of those other fancy schmancy French pastries he had pictured in his brochures. The guy was a fraud. Check out Phil's Facebook profile and you'll find the real chef behind Mr. Conman Marcel."

Leona handed the envelope with Phil's note and the recipes to Christy.

"What's this?"

"I found it in one of the crates of food the chef brought. It suggests to me that Phil was doling out recipes slowly as the chef needed them for these workshops. His patience ran out this time and he demanded payment."

"Check out the handwriting," Annie said. "The note and the recipes don't match the chef's very distinctive style." She picked up one of the many signed brochures on the floor and handed it to Christy.

"This explains a lot," Christy said. "I found a big box of recipes in Phil's car. If what Robin is saying is true, Phil was the expert and the chef needed those recipes for his book. He'd already gotten an advance and his publisher was getting impatient for the final product."

"I have to know," Robin said to Christy, "was Phil poisoned with ground up cherry pits?"

"What? Who started that rumor?"

Robin looked away as her cheeks took on a cherry red color.

Detective Crank continued, "We discovered that peanuts were added to Phil's coffee and we suspect it was the chef that put them in there."

Leona smacked her forehead. "I should have thought of that. When he sent in his paperwork, he said he had a peanut allergy. But don't most people carry an EpiPen with them?"

"Phil had one in his suitcase but from what we reconstructed, we think he panicked when the allergy symptoms began, he slid off the road, and slammed into a snowbank during the storm. The impact knocked him unconscious and he never recovered to give himself the shot."

"Ask Alex to show you a video he has on his camera from Bigger Burger," Annie said. "It should help to confirm that the chef did, in fact, add something to Phil's coffee." She hoped that was enough for Christy, since she didn't want Tricia to have to get involved. Even with everything wrapped up.

Roxy whined and pawed at Annie's leg. She bent down on one knee. "Don't worry, I'm fine." Buddy put his front paws on Annie's knee and licked her face. Trouble was determined not to be left out of all the excitement and squeezed between Roxy and Buddy.

"Any room for me?" Jason's voice whispered in her ear.

"Always." She stood and leaned against his strong body.

30

"I can't believe that sweet old lady turned out to be a love-obsessed killer," Annie's mom said as she set a scone, butter, and jam in front of her on Monday morning. "And, here, Greta and I were thinking we were holding down the fort while you and Leona got to have all the fun baking with some guests at the Blackbird." She shook her head. "Next time Leona insists she needs your help, I'm coming, too."

"And close down the Black Cat Café?"

"We'll figure something out."

Jason held up the jam jar. "Sour cherry jam? Where'd this come from?"

"Leona sent it over. She said it was in one of the crates of food that the chef brought to the Blackbird. It came with a recipe. She said if it tastes good, she might make more with the rest of the cherries."

Greta looked at the label. "What's a sour cherry?"

Annie used her knife to scoop a little of the jam from the jar. She licked it off the knife. "Oh, my goodness." Her whole face puckered into a mass of wrinkles. "This needs more sugar to be edible."

Greta laughed as she read from her phone, "Yeah, sour cherries are, well, sour and have a tendency to make you pucker if you eat them."

"So much for *that* recipe from Chef Marcel, or Conman Marcel as Robin renamed him." Annie pushed the jam away from her plate.

Alex walked into the café and looked around before he slid into the empty seat next to Annie. "I just wanted to say goodbye before leaving. I know you had your suspicions about me but it all worked out in the end. I have to tell you that I thought Leona was going to have a heart attack when we heard that crash upstairs. It was a repeat of when Chef Marcel fell out of bed and we were at the dining room table Friday night. Did she tell you what she said to me?"

Annie shook her head.

"Her exact words as she ran to the stairs were, 'If anyone hurt a hair on Annie's head they won't get out of here alive.' She's got *your* back."

Annie smiled. She felt Jason squeeze her thigh. "Yes, she does, and I've got hers, too."

Alex tapped his finger to his forehead. "Now that my job is wrapped up here, I guess I'll be on my way."

"Did you figure out exactly why Chef Marcel hired you?" Annie asked.

"Well, it was more complicated than what he originally told me. Detective Crank and I searched through all the papers from Connie's suitcase which revealed an extensive trail that she had been stalking him for quite some time using various pseudonyms. She laid out how they should be partners, in business *and* life. For some reason, she had convinced herself that the chef was in love with her; probably wishful thinking. We think the chef wanted me to figure out who the crazy person really was and how to get her out of his life."

"Wow. And Connie actually seemed to be somewhat normal .

. . until I had her cornered with the evidence spilled all over the floor of her room." Annie shook her head at the memory. "Phil's threatening letter was just bad timing on his part?"

"I guess so. The chef's scam was beginning to fall apart and when Phil demanded money, his fair share in my opinion, the chef must have panicked and decided to take care of the problem in the only way he could think of—make it look like a peanut allergy reaction."

"I owe you an apology, Alex. I had a hard time letting go of thinking you might have killed the chef. I'm glad I was wrong."

Alex grinned. "Apology accepted. Detective Crank . . . Christy . . . also thanked me for hanging around and keeping you and Leona out of trouble."

"She said that?" Annie frowned.

"She sure did. She loves to wear that tough guy image, but underneath she actually has a pretty big heart." Alex patted Annie's shoulder. "I'm on my way, but don't be surprised if you see me back in this cozy town sometime."

"Really? I thought you'd drive out with your tires squealing and without even a glance in your rearview mirror," Annie replied.

"Nope, Catfish Cove has grown on me—the quaint town atmosphere, the beautiful mountain setting, the food, and I suppose most of the people aren't too bad either." Alex elbowed Annie and grinned. He lowered his voice. "And I wouldn't mind seeing that detective again. She's dynamite."

Annie's eyes popped open. "That, she is." She was sure *she* wouldn't want to spend too much time with a lit stick of dynamite wearing a tight ponytail and a stink-eye to win a gold medal, but maybe that worked for Alex.

Camilla rushed in through the door just as Alex left the café. "Annie! Tyler just filled me in on what happened at the Blackbird. I can't believe it. That nice old lady that bought an expensive necklace from my store tried to kill you?"

"It wasn't even close, Camilla." Annie winked at Jason.

The café door jingled. Annie turned to see Leona entering. Danny followed with a package tucked carefully under his arm.

"I cancelled the baking lesson I promised the guests this morning. Everyone wanted to get going anyway and get as far away as possible from this nightmare weekend." Leona took the seat that Alex had already warmed. She put her arm around Annie and pulled her close. "I really thought there might be another murder at the Blackbird when I heard that thump yesterday."

"Yeah, Alex told me what you said, but why did you think it was me upstairs?"

Leona shook her head. "I don't know. Instinct, I guess. You always pop into my brain first. Anyway, Danny and I have something for you." She took the package from Danny and placed it in front of Annie. "Go ahead. Open it."

Annie tore off the brown paper to reveal a beautiful cherry-framed oval mirror. She turned to Leona. "For me?"

"Danny made two. I have one hanging next to the coat tree by the front door at the Blackbird and this one should hang in here. It's a magic mirror." The corners of Leona's mouth twitched. "I'll be able to see what's going on here while I'm at the bed and breakfast."

Everyone burst out laughing. "You wish!" Annie managed to say in between several loud snorts.

A NOTE FROM LYNDSEY

Thank you for reading my cozy mystery, *Cherry Buried Cake.*
    Never miss a release date and sign up for my newsletter here
—http://LyndseyColeBooks.com

ABOUT THE AUTHOR

Lyndsey Cole lives in New England in a small rural town with her husband who puts up with all the characters in her head, her dog who hogs the couch, her cat who is the boss, and 3 chickens that would like to move into the house. She surrounds herself with gardens full of beautiful perennials. Sitting among the flowers with the scent of lilac, peonies, lily of the valley, or whatever is in bloom, stimulates her imagination about who will die next!

ALSO BY LYNDSEY COLE

PoisonBuried Punch

CranBuried Coffee Cake

WineBuried Wedding

Jingle Buried Cookies

Easter Buried Eggs

Boo Buried Cupcakes

Merry Buried Christmas

CPSIA information can be obtained
at www.ICGtesting.com
Printed in the USA
LVHW111153260622
722147LV00017B/287